true

Nicole Harman

Cover design by Cory DeYonker
Edited by Stephen Zimmer
ISBN : 978-1-7358940-1(paperback)
ISBN : 978-1-7358940-5-8 (ebook)

For such a simple word, one that is easy to say and spell, a heaviness weighs upon the meaning of the word True.

It's a word we use so often in our language. It describes the difference between false and honest. The difference between real and fake.

Most everyone knows the meaning, once it's said. However, to be labeled with this word holds an entirely new weight. It means that I have to know, understand, and be this view of purity, as well as perfection.

When I discovered I was a True Sage, I didn't think much of this word. The label for my power and myself as a person had changed so quickly and so often that I didn't know what to think of the word. But as the seasons began to change from the cold, unforgiving winter, to the inviting, hopeful spring, my studies brought more and more curiosity, understanding, and, in turn, knowledge, about the rarity of being a True.

I found each day, as I watched the leaves grow on the trees outside my dorm, the label of True began to grow on me. I was finding myself increasingly in tune with both of my powers and, more importantly, how they worked together, hand in hand.

I could feel, each and every day, my power—my potential—building inside of me and growing like a wildfire, feeding off of the dry brush. The more it grew, the more I felt responsible to understand it, and to control it.

Ever since Byrein had made his intentions for me clear, I felt more determined than ever to find a way to disconnect us as much as possible. There was a sense of urgency to my day-to-day lessons: a need to learn more.

And yet, by no doing of my own, he seemed to leave me alone recently. It had been months since he last invaded my thoughts. And weeks since I had a Mind Sight episode that led to anything revolving around him. But he always stayed in the back of my mind, keeping me on guard every waking moment. He was like my own version of a mild tension headache that you could forget about at times, but never really goes away.

I found myself veering the conversation away from him more and more with Jewel. I hated how the light in her optimistic eyes would falter, ever so slightly, at the mention of him, or his followers, the Exes. Thankfully, whenever I did have to guide the conversation away from the matter, she either didn't think twice or didn't mind, though I'm not really sure which. As it was, she had plenty to focus on and keep her mind occupied.

Since the day on the beach last winter, when I connected to her power for the sake of helping Moz, I could feel Jewel's power grow more intense as well. It was altered that day. I had manipulated her power, and by doing so, the event had altered her thinking, not entirely in a bad way. She now saw how much more she could be capable of, giving her a newfound confidence. And it made way for a new set of skills for her to explore.

Just thinking of her brought a smile to my lips as I sipped my tea, gazing out my window at the golden sunrise peeking through the tree branches. It brought a calmness to the room and a feeling of hope for the morning. I played with the rim of my mug and felt the steam lick my knuckles, allowing the hopeful warmth to embrace every fiber of my being like a fuzzy blanket on a chilly day.

A rhythmic knock on my door sounded off in the quiet of the morning, and I didn't even have to turn to know that it was Jewel entering my room. She closed the door behind her, and I could feel her pause.

With a gentle surge of power leaving my bare toes, I saw Jewel's blue-eyed face come into view within my mind. She swished the orange-red streaks of her blonde hair with the back of her hand and crept toward my snack basket.

"It's not in there," I noted nonchalantly, as I pulled myself from my Sight episode.

"Huh, what?" Jewel asked.

Keeping my eyes on the outside world, I lifted a hand off my mug and pointed beside me to the small side table, where a green mug of tea sat waiting for her. Beside it was a small cookie in clear wrapping.

"You are getting scary good at that Sight power of yours," Jewel huffed as she joined me next to the window. The crinkle from the cookie's wrapping echoed around the barren walls of my dorm room.

"That's the last one, be sure to enjoy it." I chuckled before taking another sip.

From the corner of my eye, I could see Jewel take a slow, dramatic bite of the cookie and savor each and every crumb. She reminded me of Hunter eating one of my mom's muffins back in our hometown of Athra. Mornings like this made me miss the simplicity my life used to consist of.

"Thinking of Hunter today, too?" Jewel asked.

"And my mom," I noted and drank the last of my tea.

Jewel nodded with understanding. "Are you going to the academy this morning?"

"Yeah, Mr. Sean is supposed to be back from his trip to North District today. You?"

"Yep, I'm going early. My teacher wants to discuss something with me," Jewel explained, shrugging her shoulders. "She didn't exactly tell me what. Just that it has to do something with an opportunity, or something for me."

"Are you sure you're not in trouble?" I sassed.

She ticked her tongue. "I'll have you know, I have been doing great in class. Except for that one time when I splashed water all over Belleza, though at that point, I am pretty sure my instructor cracked a smile. She did kinda deserve it," Jewel defended, turning her nose up.

I scrunched my nose at the mention of Belleza and tried to imagine her perfect, long, brunette hair, stringy and wet, and clinging to her face. I shook my head. *Why does she still look pretty in my head?* Disappointed, I placed my mug on the desk and slid into shoes.

Jewel gulped down the last of her tea and came to join me by the door, seeming ready for the day. I could smell the scent of her fruity lotion still lingering on her skin as she linked arms with me, just as she always had before we set off toward the academy.

Just outside the tall academy building we paused and admired the twinkling of the moving metal sculpture on top. It was peaceful outside in the crisp morning air.

A clumping of uneven steps against the pavement echoed nearby. I turned to see the unexpected sight of Mr. Sean as he meandered his way to the academy, wearing his worn-out boots and stained, tan trench coat.

His eyes flicked to Jewel, and then me, before landing on the academy doors just ahead of us. He paused in thought and pulled a calloused hand from his trench coat pocket, running it through his greasy brown hair.

I glanced at Jewel and gave her a nod, to go on ahead of me. She smiled a silent "okay," before unlinking from my arm and entering the large doors of the academy.

"Good morning, Mr. Sean," I greeted.

"Mornin' Esmari." His eyes were tired and red. "It's quiet this mornin'. Let's do some lessons outside."

Mr. Sean brushed past me, and I knew he intended for me to follow him. Swiftly, I spun on my heel to obey.

I watched his deformed wings sway as he walked, allowing the pieces that looked like burnt black strings to be tossed back and forth in the slightest of breezes. Every so often, his wings would twitch, and I could see the muscles in his neck tense for a moment, from what I could only assume was pain. He never said a word about it.

As we arrived at the back of the academy in a grass clearing, Mr. Sean paused and pinched the bridge of his nose. *His Distance Sight is giving him headaches again. I wonder why we are working outside today.* I shrugged but held my tongue from asking. I couldn't quite read his mood yet. He took a deep breath and released his hand, once again opening his eyes.

"Today, I want you to practice your strength of touchin' my power. You need to better control it," Mr. Sean said. "But, you also need to release and work on that Sage Power, that Sage Energy of yours. Which do you want to start with?"

"Sir?" I started. Ever since he discovered that I could pause his power, essentially, he continually became interested in me learning how to control that side of my power, and I could never quite understand why. The idea of it made me anxious and uncomfortable.

"Either you pick, or I will," Mr. Sean stated coldly.

"Sage," I responded flatly.

Mr. Sean nodded. He walked a few feet from me and sat in the overgrown grass, closing his eyes and allowing his head to fall back, facing the morning sky.

I allowed my senses to take in my surroundings. I understood the feeling burning in my veins, itching to find its way from my fingertips. There was so much energy around me. I could feel all the effects of it like static electricity running along the tiny hairs of my arms. A breeze rustled through the grass at my ankles, as it played with the dew clinging to the tip of each blade.

Grasping at the feeling of pure energy surrounding me, I flicked a spark into my palm. Slowly, I allowed it to engulf my entire hand.

I held on to the feeling and watched as my power swirled and laced itself around the crooks of my fingers and made its way to my wrist. I took a breath and allowed my opposite hand to release power just the same.

I could feel my wings extending out simultaneously on my back. I breathed as my Sage Energy flowed throughout my wings at my spine, filling each of the cracks with a glowing beauty and completing their true form. A smile curled at the corner of my lip, and I allowed them to carry me into the air.

I hovered there, just for a moment, taking in the serenity of the morning air accompanied by the slight hum from the power in my hands. Allowing all other thoughts and feelings to melt away, I brought my hands together, pressing my palms against one another tightly. I could feel my hands resisting, pushing away from one another, as if they were two positive ends of a magnet.

I pressed against the sensation, attempting to remain steady and allow the orbs of power around each hand to become one. I pressed my hands firmly toward one another, attempting to convince them to coincide. I could feel a sense of tension in my shoulders as I tried to keep calm and stable.

It was too much. My hands flew away from one another, and the power sent sparks raining down to the earth below.

My wings faltered and I was sent hurtling to the ground. My only choice was to catch myself with my feet and I braced for the impact, as the ground slammed against the soles of my shoes.

"That was better than before," Mr. Sean mentioned, his voice laced with sass as he brushed the arms of his trench coat.

"Don't mock me," I said flatly.

"Now that that's out of your system," Mr. Sean noted, half under his breath.

"Yes, yes. I know," I said, shaking out my still-throbbing feet.

Mr. Sean stood with a grunt, and I made my way to him. Fear rose within me. I didn't like this part of learning my Mind Sight. I thought that maybe, after he returned from his mysterious adventure to the North District, he would leave it be. Maybe he would forget about training me on this. Maybe he would decide it wasn't necessary for me to do this at all.

That did not seem to be the case. If anything, he was almost more insistent on it than before. Then again, maybe I was just more agitated and sensitive about it.

"When you are ready, Esmari," Mr. Sean prompted impatiently. I couldn't quite tell what it was, but he seemed to have a reason for me practicing this, lingering behind his glare now.

I nodded and lifted a hand. With two fingers, I pressed gently, just below his shoulder. I felt the closeness of his power, a feeling that made me uneasy, to say the least.

I allowed myself to focus on his power. On its root. Hesitantly, I released a surge of power from my very own supply, and instantaneously connected to his power.

Feeling how it moved through his every vein, I sensed how it pained him. I felt it press willingly against my power, against my fingers. It was like the warmth from a fireplace on a cool day as it wafted toward my veins. I wanted to allow the feeling to spread. I thirsted for it.

Quickly, I yanked away. I shook my head, trying to catch my breath and gain stability once more. It wasn't exactly that I didn't like it, I just didn't like the way it made me feel after touching someone's power. It terrified me that I yearned so deeply for it.

"Again!" Mr. Sean barked.

I clenched my jaw. There were so many words I wanted to say. Anger boiled in the words forming in my throat, but I swallowed them back.

I allowed a breath to release from my flared nostrils as I stepped toward him once more. Again, I placed two fingers just below his shoulder and released a surge to connect with his power.

I could feel myself reaching closer and closer to his power. I wanted to touch it. I felt as though I needed to reach out and touch it. Connecting to his power with another release of my own, I could feel how it surged through his body. How it radiated toward his eyes. How it engulfed every fiber of his being.

I wanted it.

Thoughts of possibilities filled my head. Possibilities of what I could do. I could feel my heart beating faster. Like a terrifying rush of adrenaline.

As he closed his eyes, his painful power eased for a moment. I didn't want to lose it. It was slowly slipping from me. Like a liquid seeping through my fingers. I needed it to be more prominent. More stable. Suddenly, it was. Mr. Sean opened his eyes and allowed the power to reactivate in full force.

I yanked away, startled, and in doing so, I found myself releasing an unintentional surge of power like a jolt of electricity. We both staggered away from each other at the force of the disconnect. I gasped as if I had forgotten to breathe.

Mr. Sean clenched his jaw. His hand flew to his head, pressing a palm to his temple, and he looked around bewildered for a moment. He didn't speak, and I didn't dare to either. *Please don't make me try again.* My face flushed with a mix of embarrassment and lingering adrenaline.

My eyes stayed on Mr. Sean. After what felt like minutes, he stood and tucked his hands inside his pockets, taking a long deep breath. He nodded to himself.

"Good," he said.

I searched his face for more of an answer. His eyes looked glazed over, as if he were lost in his own world. I didn't dare speak.

"Let's move inside," Mr. Sean requested and began walking toward the academy without waiting for an answer from me.

two

We entered the towering double doors of the academy. It was quiet inside, though it was still rather early for most classes. The way the light glistened against the tile flooring gave a sense of humble hope to the space before us.

There was comfort in the familiarity of the space, and something about the recent change in warmer weather filled my soul with serenity.

Mr. Sean sighed beside me, as if dissatisfied

with the surroundings. His shoulders sank ever so slightly, and he shoved his hands deep into the pockets of his tan trench coat.

"Good morning! I was just on my way to find you two," echoed a deep, distinguished voice from the top of the stairs. Mr. Higgens' gleaming face appeared with a glistening agenda behind his deep brown eyes. He tossed his glossy new cane under his arm, and leaned heavily against the railing, as he made his way down the dark wooden planks of the stairs to meet us at the bottom.

That explains Mr. Sean's demeanor. I eyed Mr. Sean. He wasted no energy on hiding his discontentment. I turned back toward Mr. Higgens, who tightened his grip on the intricately carved walking cane, pressing it firmly against the ground. Every few steps, his wings would flick on his back, as if to prompt him along, despite his limp.

"Good morning, Mr. Higgens," I greeted, allowing a soft smile to form on my lips. I felt a tingle on my skin as I sensed the presence of the power radiating from Mr. Higgens before me. Quietly, I hushed the feeling.

Mr. Higgens smirked. "I have something to ask of you two. Something of a proposition, I suppose."

"Not interested," Mr. Sean scoffed, turning away and stepping toward the hall.

"But you haven't even heard what it is," Mr. Higgens prompted. I watched as he raised a gray eyebrow at Mr. Sean.

"No," Mr. Sean stated plainly.

Mr. Higgens took a sigh and turned toward me. "Esmari, there is a festival coming up, one that North District and the Ruling Family of Banshui puts on every few years. It's quite a tradition and a big to-do! It's called 'The Regal Festival.' Those in charge of putting on the festival have requested for us to have a couple of our students present their talents and abilities during the festival again this year. I've spoken with them, and we all agree that we would like for you to be one of the presenters at the festival. What do you say?"

"I—" I didn't know what to think of the offer.

"See, I was right. Not interested," Mr. Sean growled. My ears became hot.

"Sean—"

"No!" Mr. Sean's voice boomed with annoyance, cutting off Mr. Higgens. He ran his calloused hand through his greasy hair.

"Sean, I think this would be a great opportunity

for her," Mr. Higgens stated, stamping his cane down. He flashed a look at me with an encouraging twinkle in his eye. "Well?"

"It does sound intriguing—" I started.

"I am her teacher, and I say no!" Mr. Sean interrupted, sneering.

"Well, I am the Head of this Academy, and I say yes. Plus, they requested Esmari—*by name.* So, it's settled!" Mr. Higgens flicked his eyebrows at me with satisfaction, the wrinkles of his cheeks growing deeper as the smile spread across his lips. He gave me a definitive nod and turned to stride down the hall, opposite where we were headed.

I guess you just agreed to it, Esmari. I glanced at my feet for a moment, allowing a quiet breath to leave my lips. The word "requested" lingered in my mind.

My eye darted to Mr. Sean, who threw a hand up, exasperated. I could feel the frustration emanating from where he stood, tainting the morning air.

"You are just putting her on display for *anyone* to see!" Mr. Sean called. He pinched at his brow for a moment before grunting and clumping away in his grungy boots.

I didn't know what else to do but to follow. Mr. Sean didn't even take time to glance back at me, by the time we made it to the Sight classroom, clear in the back of the school. He scuffed his feet against the brick flooring as he walked in.

I could hear him grumble something to himself as he entered his office and nearly slammed the door shut. *Guess you are on your own this morning, Es.*

I tucked a stray strand of bland, sand-colored hair behind my ear and began studying the book that lay open on the wood podium. The light radiating through the windows was magical this morning as it danced across the pages I read.

I became lost in the words I was reading, which were so eloquently written, unlike most of the other books in this library of Sight power knowledge. The writer was telling from experiences with passion and emotion, not in an informative book style. There were opinions and praises, and loads of encouragement, something I lacked from my teacher.

Before I knew it, it was time for lunch. I glanced over at the door to Mr. Sean's office to find it still closed. I pursed my lips together and took a quick sigh, before heading toward the cafeteria.

My feet knew the way, and I followed mindlessly through the halls. An echoing chatter graced the hall with life. A picture here or a poster there would catch my eye as I walked, providing entertainment along the journey.

"Hey, Es!" called Jewel, as she waved her arm excitedly above her head, rounding the corner.

"Great timing," I noted, with a smirk.

Jewel was grinning from ear to ear, not usually something I saw her do when coming from classes. I raised my eyebrows and gave a quick nod to her, silently prompting her to share what had gotten her so excited. She opened her mouth to answer, just as her stomach let out a large growl. I allowed a chuckle to leave my lips.

She giggled. "I'll tell you over lunch." Quickly, she linked an arm with me and pulled me inside the cafeteria doors.

The well-lit room before us smelled of a mix of delicious foods, presenting a sense of warmth and happiness to our nostrils. The tables around the room were decorated with new, elegant, satin tablecloths in a multitude of shades of pastel colors. Fresh floral arrangements were placed at the center of each table in crystal vases, bringing the essence of the spring season indoors.

Jewel and I acquired our lunches. I chose a turkey avocado sandwich and a mango juice. After remembering to grab a green apple for Mr. Sean, we took our seats at one of the tables on the far end of the cafeteria. There was a moment of peaceful bliss as we began eating our food.

I found myself admiring my friend beside me, happy to just have her in my life. It was a moment that I could tell was fleeting, wafting away like steam from a hot meal. I wasn't sad about it, just aware.

"So, are you going to tell me what has you so excited or not?" I prodded, lifting my juice to my lips.

"Oh, right!" Jewel nodded. She finished her bite and set down the roll in her hands. Gently, she dusted the crumbs over her plate and turned to face me. "Okay, so you know how I had come to the academy with you early today—well of course you know, you were there—anyway, my teacher wanted to talk to me. Well, she had an idea for me—more than an idea, I suppose. More of a proposition—no, no, that's not the word—opportunity! That's the word I am looking for. She has an opportunity for me!"

I chuckled softly at her. "Okay, what is the opportunity?"

Jewel rambled with excitement, "Well, I have been improving a lot lately, she said, and I guess she heard about me helping with Moz on the beach, you know with the poison and his leg. I had sorta mentioned wanting to really start expanding my abilities, doing something more with them, something more with my life, you know, like long term. So, I guess she reached out to the local medical offices and infirmaries and such, and she said there are some people interested in taking me under their wing. I apparently 'could have a future' with this."

"Jewel! That's great! So, are you going to go for it? I mean are you going to take that opportunity?" I asked.

Her shoulders dropped. "I don't know—I mean—I guess—I don't know—" Jewel's face became clouded with anxiety.

"What do you mean 'I don't know?' You were so excited about it a second ago, and now not so much. It sounds like a fantastic opportunity for you! One with a promising future," I encouraged.

Jewel rambled again, lost in thought. "Yes, but

it means leaving everything I know behind at the academy. And moving on—and making choices—and I guess I will still be doing some classes and stuff—and I will still be around sorta—and I will just be observing, not really making the big choices—"

"So, it sounds like it is just going to take the place of some of your studies for now. Just think of it as a new class, just not at the academy," I noted.

Jewel nodded. "You're right! Flitters, you certainly know how to make me more confident sometimes, Es."

I chuckled. "Me? Make *you* more confident?" I shook my head and took another bite.

"So, what about your morning? How's the long-lost teacher?" Jewel asked, once again retrieving her roll from her plate. She eyed me slyly.

"He wasn't lost. He just went on a trip. And he's just as determined and moody as ever." I sighed.

Jewel flashed me a sorrowful frown before changing the topic. "Mr. Higgens seemed chipper this morning when he visited our classroom."

"I saw him in the hall this morning too." I said, nodding. "He is excited about The Regal Festival."

"Oh! Oh! I completely forgot that was coming up!" Jewel exclaimed, bouncing in her seat. "It's so much fun, Es! They have presentations and competitions. Oh, and vendors of all sorts. And there's music and dancing. And you get to see the Ruling family. But the most fun part is that you get to dress up! Not just look nice, but you get to wear fancy ball gowns and pretty shoes and such. It's such a big to do! It's sort of a tradition to dress all up. We just *have* to make time for going."

"I—" I began.

Jewel continued, "Oh, we will need to go shopping for our dresses together. I think a good amount of the fun is trying them all on. But when you find that one that just fits you and makes you feel your best—I am not taking no for an answer! We need to go to the festival."

"Jewel, I was asked to present," I finally managed to say.

"You were asked? Like they requested you?" Jewel's blue eyes sparkled with awe.

"By name, apparently." I sighed. Just thinking of how important the festival was starting to sound, made me nervous that I would not be what they hoped.

"Wow. I mean, just, wow!" Jewel breathed. "That's so interesting. I mean, I know they invite people, but this is so cool!"

"Interesting is definitely the word I used. It seems interesting, but what am I even supposed to present? What power are they expecting to see from me? I mean, my Mind Sight is just that, in my mind. How do I display that?" I asked. Anxiety was begging to set in, the more I thought of it.

" —and they thought I would be a perfect fit for one of their presenters this year." Belleza's voice beckoned in the cafeteria like an unwelcome shrill, making my jaw clench. I felt a tinge of anger race through my shoulders and to the tip of my wings, as they twitched against the chair's back. I glanced to see her and Lilly striding into the room. "I mean, I am not all that surprised. My daddy did say that they have had an eye on me for this year's festival. So, when Mr. Higgens asked to talk to me, I just knew what it was about."

I could see Lilly smile at her best friend, as if excited for her, but an envious longing lingered in her eyes. "That's so exciting for you, Lezzy."

I peered back at Jewel. *Great. I get to be a fellow presenter with the one and only Belleza.*

Jewel seemed to understand my gaze and nodded. She pressed her lips together, as if unsure what to say. I waited for a quirky remark or a backhanded comment, but Jewel just looked at the food before her and took another bite.

"I hear they are asking only a couple of us students. I think Mr. Higgens said it was two of us from the academy. I bet they will ask Kasius," Belleza continued, as she passed our table.

"You two would be wonderful presenters together." Lilly smiled hopefully. "I heard Mr. Higgens say earlier today that he has already confirmed one promising presenter that is sure to wow."

"He must have already talked to Kasius then. I can't think of anyone else that would fit that description," Belleza noted smugly.

Jewel flicked me a glance, raising her eyebrows. I shook my head at her and rolled my eyes as I removed the toothpick from the second half of my sandwich and placed it aside on my plate.

I allowed myself to watch from the corner of my eye as Belleza and Lilly took a seat nearby. Even the way they relaxed into their chairs was irritating and full of ego. Belleza daintily pulled apart a croissant with the tips of her fingers and ate it piece by piece, careful not to smudge her rose-colored lipstick.

She glanced across the room, as if judging the others around her. Another person joined, and she greeted them with a welcoming nod. It was as if she needed to grant them permission, and as if they felt obligated to look for the permission in the first place.

I let a sigh escape my lips and turned my attention back to the food before me. Jewel had already moved on and chatted about a silly occurrence she had seen when she visited her parents the other day. It was, from my understanding, quite an unusual circumstance. I listened and provided a smile or nod every so often, while we finished our lunch.

When I returned to the classroom after lunch, Mr. Sean was still locked away in his office. I was not entirely surprised, but some part of me hoped he wouldn't be. That he would provide me with some sort of instruction or wild idea to try.

Instead, I studied on my own the rest of the afternoon, only occasionally hearing a grunt of frustration, or the pound of a book being tossed out of use.

three

I walked the halls of the academy as a gentle, golden yellow glow seeped inside the windows. There was something about the dust as it wafted in the rays of light that was so mystical. I found myself lost in the moment as I meandered my way outside.

Recently, I had given myself much more time to just be. To breathe and to live. To explore and take my time.

So much of my studies seemed to be in a rush,

as though Mr. Sean needed me to learn as quickly as possible. It was frantic at times and incohesive. Often feeling like he didn't truly know the correct way to get me to the lesson he needed me to learn. But, when I wasn't with him, when it wasn't class time, I wanted to take a moment to slow down.

I especially liked my walks at the end of the afternoon, lately. The halls were usually on the quiet side. Most students had left for the day. Some instructors would still be around preparing for the following day's lessons. But there generally wasn't any chatter. No small talk to engage in. No glances to avoid. No expectations to uphold. At least, not at this hour.

I opened the doors of the academy and took in a breath of the still-warm afternoon air before I exited for the day. My mind wandered to what being a presenter meant for this upcoming festival. *What do I have to offer? What could be interesting to see from me?* I didn't feel like heading to the dorm just yet. I wanted to enjoy the afternoon for just a little longer.

Mindlessly, my feet led me to a tree, and I sat against the trunk, allowing a soft smile to fall upon my lips. A gentle nagging at the nape of my neck urged as the soft blades of grass brushed against my legs. Softly, I slid out of my sandal and gripped the warm grass between my toes, gently releasing a surge of power.

A woman within a shop sat sewing tiny beads to the sleeve of a mint-colored dress. The design glittered in the light that hung, swaying slightly, just overhead. Every so often, she would sit back and admire her work, tossing the fabric into a better position, so that she could continue. I remained there, watching her, as she intricately created, peaceful in the space. A dainty chime on her door sounded off. She didn't so much as glance up at them.

"We're closed for the day, come back tomorrow," she called.

There were a couple of footsteps before she glanced up. Her face changed. Flustered, she set the dress down. She pressed her chair away from the workspace in a rush.

"Oh, I'm sorry, please do come in!" she welcomed happily.

The woman faded from view, and I sat still for a moment as I waited for the world around me to return to my gaze. It slowly seeped in as I observed the sounds accompanying it. A rustle in the new leaves of the trees graced my ears and the cool breeze in the air kissed my skin. I felt a power present with me.

Quietly, someone was watching. I looked around in the space near me through the fading light as the sun was nearly set. Placing my fingers on my necklace, I felt, as the black onyx and jade stones hung side by side on the dinging silver chain.

The individual, seeming satisfied, softly walked away. They stood tall, with one hand tucked in their pocket. There was no mistaking the figure. *Kasius, you were watching over me again, weren't you?* I felt a warmth in my chest as I watched him walk away, grateful for his protective nature. I got up and brushed myself off for a moment, enjoying the last of the sunset as it dipped out of sight.

"Hey Es!" Jewel's voice rang.

I turned to see my friend emerging from the shadows just as the walkway lights flickered on. Quickly, I raised my hand and offered a warm, silent, hello.

"I'm headed to the Dripping Crown to help out for a bit. Want to tag along and grab a coffee? My treat?" Jewel offered.

I thought for a moment. "Sure, that sounds

nice," I replied. My head still felt a bit foggy from my Mind Sight episode.

Jewel seemed to notice too but didn't say anything about it. She flicked open her iridescent wings and fluttered up into the sky without looking back for me. I smirked to myself slyly and glided up into the evening sky after her.

With a flick of my fingers, I summoned a marble of Energy into my palm and felt my wings fill out behind me. The glow from my wings glinted off the edges of Jewel's wings. Carefully, I flapped my wings and zoomed past her.

"Stop showing off, you Sage!" Jewel teased with a chuckle.

I circled back and joined her for a moment, flittering below her before returned to her side. She reached out with a gentle hand and pushed me playfully at my shoulder as she rolled her eyes dramatically. I flashed her a big, goofy grin.

The lights on the streets and buildings created a glow that spread across the Central District and seeped into Coastal District as we arrived on the rustic front porch of the Dripping Crown. I watched as the sign for the store teetered back and forth on the hinges, swaying in the salty breeze from the beachfront. With a crank of the creaking metal handle, we entered.

It was a busy night for the little coffee shop. Busier than I had seen in quite a while. There was chatter from groups of people all around, just loud enough that the chime from the bell hanging over the door was barely noticed.

A large group of ladies were holding what looked like a book club upstairs in the loft, where we usually sat when we came in. I glanced at the bar seats and spotted one toward the middle.

"Jewels!" Victor called out. He adjusted his wire-rimmed glasses and the worn, navy blue cap on his head. "Thanks for coming! Grab an apron!"

"Coming!" Jewel called back. She skipped to the counter and slid the neck strap of the black apron over her head. She quickly looped the ties around her waist, before scrubbing her hands clean in the sink. Soon, she was working away at a list of drinks, as happy as ever.

I took a seat at the barstool I had seen before and contently watched the commotion around me. A few minutes later, Jewel came and brought me a latte in a large green mug. She had attempted to make a flower in the foam, though it kinda looked like an umbrella. Grateful, I took it.

"I'm working on the art, it's not too good yet, but I'm starting to get the hang of it!" Jewel chipperly noted.

I smiled and took a sip of the sweet coffee. A few people around me left and made room for others to sit soon after. I listened in on the chatter of two older men nearby, as they discussed the weather. From my understanding, it was not to the liking of either man, being that the wind was more prominent at night than it used to be. A couple of women came downstairs with books in hand and eagerly discussed what was to come in the next chapter.

"Busy night here," I observed aloud to Victor as he wiped down the counter beside me and collected the recently departed guest's dirty mug.

"I'd say so! I don't mind the busyness. It's usually like this when the weather starts to warm up. Everyone is eager to go and do things again. Now that the snow has all melted, that is." Victor smiled and wiped the counter down once more, just as a chime from the bell on the door sounded, allowing for another customer to enter. "Hello! Welcome!"

A prickle danced across the hair on my arms. The feeling I got when I am around someone of a significant amount of power. A power I am not used to feeling.

I breathed in the exhilarating feeling of curiosity. This power nearby me was different from so many others around me, but in what way? I couldn't quite figure it out, which made me even more intrigued to understand it as it passed behind me.

The individual ordered their coffee, and I could feel their presence and their power became more obvious. The person sat beside me quietly and I glanced in their direction. It was a man, just maybe five or so years older than me. His build reminded me so much of my brother Bray, strong with a sturdy frame. He sat dignified, with an expression on his face that was almost dissatisfied, bored of the world around him. He was someone not to be bothered.

Jewel brought his coffee and the man said nothing, just nodded. It was the least amount of interaction someone could offer without coming off as blatantly rude. Though, I did not get a sense that this man was rude by nature, but rather became a part of his presence due to something out of his control. I could tell he didn't wish to be.

His hand met the coffee cup, and for a moment I saw it. His essence of his power. It resided in the palm of his hand. But something wasn't right about it. Like it was off in some sort of way, as if there was a conflict within the power radiating in his palm.

He lifted the cup to his lips and took a sip, and I peeled my eyes away, making sure I didn't stare for long. I blew gently on my coffee before taking a silent sip, watching as the foam swirled away from the rim of the cup.

I suddenly felt self-conscious, knowing that I was being watched. I turned sharply, to meet the eyes of the man beside me. His gaze was unwavering. He intended for me to know he was looking. It was unsettling, but something about his aqua eyes made me pause. They were like the waves I had watched so many times at the beach here in Banshui. Deep, mysterious, full of a story yet to be told.

I didn't know what to say. I didn't feel scared, just confused. Like I was caught doing nothing of particular interest. The way I used to feel when I waited outside the shops for my mom when she ran errands. I wasn't doing anything wrong, but I felt like I should have some other purpose, other than just waiting and existing.

I could tell the odd feeling in the interaction was felt by him as well. He seemed conflicted in his soul, much like the power that resided in his body and lay dormant on his palm. As if something was prompting him to interact, to address me, and something else was stopping him.

It was clear that he was aware of who I was. He didn't have to ask. I could tell just from his eyes. The way he looked upon my face and directly back into my eyes. He knew. He also didn't seem satisfied, or dissatisfied. Just neutral. Waiting. Wanting me to know he was there. Wanting me to know that he was aware.

I didn't know what to make of it. But my mind just kept going back to his power. I craved to know it. To reach for it. Knowing very well that I shouldn't. I just wanted to understand it. To quench this curiosity that danced within my head, taunting me.

I turned away first. Looking back at the cup before me and the little ring it left on the countertop. It took everything in me to fight the desire to look back into the man's eyes. I felt his gaze return forward as well, and that was that.

Neither of us said a word to one another, but I couldn't help but want to.

four

It was late by the time I left the Dripping Crown. The interesting man had left nearly an hour before me, without so much as another glance or even a head nod in my direction, taking his unfamiliar power with him. The whole encounter was peculiar, but then again, most people who know who I am act at least a little odd around me.

Before I left, however, I happened to glance down upon the seat where the man had sat beside me. A small, green leaf sat waiting, as if it were placed for me to find. My curiosity got the better of me, and I couldn't help but take it along with me as I left.

When I arrived back in my own dorm, I kicked off my shoes and flopped onto my bed. Taking a sigh, I retrieved the leaf from its hiding place in my pocket and flicked on my light.

The leaf was an unusual one. Not like those of the trees around the dorms. It was small, being no bigger than my pinky finger, and fresh too. The waxy texture of it made the leaf seem fake, like it was made of plastic and polished to be shiny.

I watched as the glossy finish glistened in the light. Gingerly, I held it up, allowing the veins of the leaf to show through, and thought once more of the odd man before turning the leaf over in my fingertips to look at the bottom side.

A soft gasp left my lips as I looked over the leaf once more. While the top of the leaf was fresh and full of life, the bottom of the leaf was completely opposite. It looked brown and dried up, ready to fall apart at any given moment. Carefully, I spun the leaf by the small stem in my fingertips, watching it flash from green to brown, green to brown. Faster and faster. Until—

Poof.

The leaf spontaneously combusted with a small pop sound, followed by a scant puff of dusty smoke. Watching through the warm lighting in my dorm room, my shoulders lowered in slight disappointment.

I looked at my now leafless hand, not knowing what to make of it. *Was that meant to happen? Or did it react with me?* I allowed my curious mind to wander as I drifted off to sleep.

———

I found my mind still thinking of that leaf over the next couple of days. It would be at the most unexpected moments that a faint memory of the puff of smoke the leaf caused would scurry into my thoughts.

I discovered this to be the case once again as I strolled the halls of the academy, waiting to meet with Jewel after her classes. It was something to keep my mind preoccupied at least. Something more than my own power and the ever-growing urgency in Mr. Sean's lessons.

A sound caught my ear, and I glanced up to notice that I had wandered down a hall I hadn't traveled often. In fact, there were many halls I hadn't ventured down, being that they were of no use to me and didn't have a destination that directly benefited my efforts.

But today was different. Today I had time to spare. Mr. Sean had already dismissed me from my lessons for the day and I, for once, was waiting on Jewel. So, I took it upon myself to think of that very leaf and meander through the academy's many halls.

Again, I heard the sound that caught my ear. It was a small jingle. So light, so dainty. It reminded me of the tiny bells that were once sewn to the bows I wore in my hair as a little girl.

Every day when I was little, my mother would gently brush my hair into whatever hairstyle she and I decided on for the day. Then she would make a big to-do about adding the "finishing touch," which was always a small hairbow with those tiny bells. And I simply loved them.

Hearing the sound brought warmth to my chest, giving me the smallest sliver of a memory of my home and my family back in Athra. I looked around for a source and was greeted by a classroom door propped wide open. Cautious not to disturb the lesson taking place inside, I quietly took a step closer and watched from a respectable distance, out in the hall.

An instructor sat up on a tabletop at one side of the classroom observing, swinging their legs out of habit. They motioned for a student to come closer. I heard the creak from the wood on an aged chair and Kasius stepped into view. He looked tense, with a face of stone, as always.

"When you are ready," said the instructor.

Kasius lifted a hand gingerly. With a twitch of his finger, I saw a glinting silver bell roll across a nearby table. His face didn't change expression. He didn't seem proud of himself. He didn't even seem fazed by the task at hand. It was just that to him. A task. Something to complete and be done.

The instructor peered back at him and nodded, not quite satisfied either. I could see them considering their words carefully.

Finally, they took a breath. "That was well done. However, I'd really like to see you apply your power—"

Kasius shook his head. "Sir, we have spoken

about this."

"All I am asking for is for you to be willing to exercise your strength today," the instructor urged calmly. "One object today. One *larger* object. I know you prefer to focus on your precision, but strength and precision are equally important. Precision helps to harness and focus while strength helps to—"

"Overpower," Kasius finished.

They took a sigh. "What if one day you need to use that strength for something larger? Not just a bell or an object that fits in your hand. It's like a muscle. You could injure yourself if you don't condition your power. Work your way up, and use it on larger, heavier objects," The instructor stated.

I allowed a small puff of air to leave my lips as I watched Kasius think his actions through. He rolled up the sleeves of his button-down shirt as he considered. I could see a breath leave his lungs as his shoulders rose and fell. Carefully, he tucked a hand in his pocket and nodded.

"Just one time, Sir," Kasius agreed, holding his free hand up.

With a gentle waft of his hand, as if he were brushing away a piece of lint floating in the air, the sizable table once holding the small bell screeched from one end of the classroom to the complete opposite side, toward the wall by the doorway. Kasius' hand snapped into a fist, and the table stopped, just before colliding with the wall.

"Your power has gotten stronger," his instructor commented.

I shifted my weight and Kasius caught sight of me. I could see in his eyes that he never intended me to see this. It seemed that he didn't intend for many to see it. He wasn't angry, but I did see the slightest tinge of remorse hiding within his gaze.

"I really wish you would trust me enough to show me the strength of your power in full. But it seems that you are at the very least exercising and conditioning your power on your own," the instructor noted. "Alright let's continue with what we were working on yesterday. Maybe tomorrow you can help me to guide some of the other students during our open lab."

Kasius turned away without a word and disappeared around the corner. I allowed myself a final breath before heading back to the main lobby.

A few moments later, Jewel joined me in a huff. She seemed frazzled and out of sorts. More than normal, that is.

She adjusted the cover of her notebook, just before tucking it in the shoulder bag she had brought with her for the day. Just as she went to close it, a pen dropped out. She let out an unsatisfied breath and bent down to snatch the pen from the floor, only to then have a crumpled-up paper drop out from her bag.

"Oh, my flutters!" Jewel exclaimed in frustration. Quickly, she gathered her items and shoved them abruptly into her bag. Standing, she gave me a nod.

"You ready?" I asked teasingly.

She rolled her eyes. "Let's fly out before something else decides to escape from my bag!"

I chuckled at her as she rushed out the door ahead of me. Jewel adjusted her strap securely on her shoulder before spreading her wings. A giddy grin spread across her face and excitement glinted in her wide blue eyes.

I laughed. "You seem excited!"

Jewel rambled, "I have been looking forward to this for the whole, entire day. It's time to go shopping! I cannot wait to try on all sorts of pretty dresses. We simply *have to* look our best for this festival. Especially now that you are going to be a presenter there for none other than the Ruling family. It's such an honor. And such a wonderful excuse to dress up and look better than ever!"

In all honesty, I wasn't sure I was in the mood to be trying on any dresses today. But it was evident that Jewel was well-prepared to shop. Her spirits were high, and hope emanated from her very presence. I watched as she flittered into the sky just before me. I followed, admiring her excitement and eagerness for the afternoon to come.

It wasn't long before we landed at the doorstep of a shop, suspended high up in the sky. Jewel smoothed her shirt down and tucked a stray hair behind her ear and out of her face. A light breeze toyed with the edges of my wings while I took a moment to look around.

I tucked my wings behind me. I couldn't help but feel a bit of anxiety shopping today. It felt odd for some reason, shopping for something like this without my mom. I hadn't seen her or shopped with her in such a long time, but today I felt like she should be here with us. Be here with me. To guide me on what would look good, or what colors would complement me best. It just felt incomplete, not being able to bring her along for shopping today.

"You okay, Es?" Jewel asked.

"Yeah, I was just thinking of my mom. Are you ready to start our shopping adventure?" I asked, flashing Jewel a reassuring smile.

She nodded with confidence. *I guess that's just part of growing up, Es. Doing things like this without your mom.* Honestly, it was bound to happen eventually, I just wished it wasn't today. I took one last breath and took a mental note to write a letter to her later, before stepping inside.

It was a sophisticated store. A few displays of dresses out front, followed by a dividing wall. Jewel walked in, starry-eyed and gleeful. I watched her take in the sight before us. My eye caught the glinting fabric from a bright pink one, and I fought everything in me not to turn my nose up at it or make a face. I didn't want to be disrespectful, but it certainly didn't suit my taste.

"Hello, how may I help you today?" a store associate called as she came from behind the dividing wall.

"We are interested in trying on some dresses for the upcoming festival," Jewel stated proudly.

"Wonderful. I only have one dressing room available at the moment, so who would I be fitting first?" the woman asked. Her silky brown hair was twisted up in a bun, held together by a fancy white-cased pen, and I watched her sophisticated, posh, mannerisms. She smoothed her sleeves down, just before pulling a measuring tape from her breast pocket on her powder-blue, button-down blouse, which looked as if it were made specifically for her features.

Jewel looked at me for a moment, and I knew how eager she was to try on her first dress. I pressed her a step forward with a gentle palm. "My friend Jewel will go first," I said to the woman with a soft smile.

The associate nodded and led us behind the partition walls where the store seemed to double in size. There were lots of colors of fabric, but all the gowns seemed to have a similar style.

Jewel stepped aside with the woman to be measured and I wandered through the dresses, not sure what I was looking for. I toyed with some of the fabric as I also kept Jewel in mind.

The woman whisked past me a few minutes later and snagged a dark blue dress from the rack, then a bright red one. I glanced over at Jewel, and she had a couple more dresses in her hands. I couldn't help but feel overwhelmed and out of place.

It wasn't long before Jewel had been set up in a dressing room and began trying on the gowns. I found a comfy seat on a nearby chair and waited to provide my advice on the many pieces she was ready to try on.

A light breeze blew down my neck from the air conditioning coming through the vents, and a slow tinge pinched at my veins. Careful of my surroundings, I flicked a small spark at the tip of my nail and toyed with it along my fingers, as if twirling a pen. The shop attendant eyed me judgmentally, but I didn't pay her rude looks any mind.

"Okay, so," Jewel started, as she emerged from the dressing room curtain. She stepped out in a peachy orange gown. "I'm not sure."

I looked her over in the cotton floor-length gown and shook my head.

"Yeah, not the best color for me," Jewel noted.

"The fabric clings in odd areas," I added.

She turned back and forth, and I watched her eyes widen as she saw where it clung to her figure. Decidedly, she went back into the dressing room to try on the next dress.

Several dresses later, she still didn't have any luck finding something we both thought suited her. Though, I thought the deep blue dress she tried on was a nice color for her.

I was fairly surprised just how different each dress looked on her figure, being that when they hung from the hanger, they looked almost identical. They were all except for the fabric, which the sales associate noted would "make or break the dress for someone." I didn't quite understand the concept behind it, but I must say that she wasn't wrong.

Jewel began to thumb through a couple more dresses on the racks and I stood for a moment to stretch. The colors of dresses and textures of fabric felt constricting as they sat on the racks, and I hadn't even tried any on yet. I rubbed at the knot forming at the nape of my neck, well aware that any amount of massaging wouldn't ease this type of tension.

"I'm going to try on a couple more, and then I'll help you grab a few dresses. Why don't you use your Sight to look around? Could help relax you a bit," Jewel suggested.

I nodded and found myself an open wall to lean my back against while I sat on the cool floor. Gently, I allowed my knuckles to dust the clean tiles below me as I released a small surge of power, enabling my Mind Sight to take over.

five

About two hours later, we had visited several more shops and still didn't find just the right dress for either of us. Jewel must have tried on over fifty dresses by this point and had a few options that she liked, but she wasn't completely sure about them for one reason or another. I thought they all looked very nice on her dainty figure.

I, on the other hand, had only tried on a handful of dresses. I wasn't sure how to pick a dress for me.

In all honesty, I had never had to dress so formally for any occasion back in Athra and was beginning to feel the pressure of choosing the correct gown.

I remembered that as a child I would read stories of people who would dress up in fancy ball gowns and meet their one true love. They would instantly find the perfect gown, or have it found for them. They would attend lavish parties and talk fancy. They would become a whole new person in the fancy attire and live happily ever after.

But Athra was not like one of those places from my childhood stores. We wore practical attire. Simple and casual. And while here in Banshui was defiantly more sophisticated and formal on the daily than in Athra, it still was no place to be in formal, floor-length ball gowns day in and day out. So, this was an entirely new concept for me. One which was more complex than I thought and full of stress.

I was finding that a truly perfect gown was so much more of a difficult task than selecting a t-shirt to throw on in the morning. Deep down, I think I had hoped that it would be a simple and quick shopping experience. Instead, my eyes were opened to all the details that were involved with my particular dress. What would be the right look? That will not only be practical for me to present in, but also make me look distinguished and respectable, all the while being something that makes me feel confident and suit me and my style?

All the dresses I seemed to try on made me either feel like I was trying too hard to look fancy, or like if I moved too quickly, I would be exposed in all the immodest ways, if I wasn't careful. The unfortunate thing was that, when I found a dress that at least fit me well, it would be in some random color like neon yellow, which didn't suit me well.

It made me wonder if I could find someone to adjust the color for me, but most of the dresses were quite pricey, and final sale. Being so, I was warned by a kind shop owner that sometimes these fabrics aren't as easily manipulated as regular clothing garments, and it could ruin the dress, and waste my money. Plus, as she put it, the designers of the dress have the gown a certain color for a reason. Seemed silly to me, but I certainly didn't want to throw my money away.

Jewel led us into another shop just as an orange glow seeped across the Central District from the evening sun. The hair on the back of my neck prickled, just for a moment. I could feel a presence, their eyes on me, but I didn't feel threatened. I just felt observed. The same way one feels when teaching a new task to a peer. I released a breath of the early evening air and the feeling disappeared along with it.

We stepped just inside the shop, catching a whiff of the freshly painted trim by the doorway, and were greeted by a kind man's warm smile. He nodded a hello to us while he finished placing a garment bag in a young woman's arms. The soft expression of her face looked familiar as she passed by. *I think she goes to the academy.* I found myself flicking a polite smile of acknowledgment while I stepped out of her way for the door.

This shop was more peaceful than the others. More relaxed in a way. There was pretty art on the walls and cozy rugs on the flooring. The lights weren't as bright and harsh as other stores, either, which I found to be something I was thankful for. Jewel got right to work, thumbing through the gowns on the rack, I, however, was feeling run down and discouraged about looking for any more dresses for myself. Instead, I wandered behind Jewel, commenting on the fabrics and colors.

"Hello, ladies!" rang the voice of the kind man.

His smile was genuine, and his eyes sparkled at the potential of two new clients. "Shopping for some gowns to wear to the upcoming festival, I take it?"

"Yes, and we haven't had a whole lot of luck yet," Jewel mentioned. "But I want my gown to be just right."

The man nodded and rested a hand on his hip. "Well, unfortunately, I didn't get my new stock like I was supposed to from our local designers this morning, so the pickin's are low, as they say. I should get them later this week. In fact, don't be too discouraged. I know most of us Central District local shops will be receiving new gowns over the next few weeks for those looking for a dress. So, you could always check back again. That's to say if we don't find you the perfect something today."

Jewel nodded happily. "Great!"

The man took a small piece of paper from his pocket and a fancy pen. "What's your name, so I can set up your dressing room?"

Jewel smiled. "I'm Jewel, and this is Esmari."

"My name is Glen, I'm the owner of this shop. I am looking forward to helping you ladies!" Glen said chipperly, as he jotted down our names in blue ink.

I watched as he walked across to the fitting room doors and clipped our name cards onto the brassy clamps fastened on the center of each door. He nodded and smoothed at his sleeves, and I watched as his wings twitched at his back. They looked satin and shone with a charcoal to navy gradient, complimented with silver accented edges. I observed again as he adjusted his wings against his back and caught a glimpse of a Royal's mark.

"Okay, I see that you have a couple of dresses in hand already, love. But if I could maybe make a suggestion? Put back that purple, it is not at all right for you." Glen shrugged. "Instead, let's maybe pull—this one—and this one—and maybe this."

He gently took the dresses from Jewel's hand and led her over to the fitting room he had set up for her. She entered and closed the door behind her, and Glen turned to me, studying me carefully with his eyes.

"Now, what should we put you in?" he thought aloud.

"I think I am all dressed out today." I sighed.

Glen ticked his tongue, shaking his head. "I think let's try this on—and maybe a blue—or maybe a plumb." He gathered a couple of options. "You came to shop, so let's find some options. Better yet, let's narrow down what doesn't work on you."

I reluctantly agreed.

"Okay, how's this one?" Jewel called as she came out in the first gown, a bright pink one, with no shape to it.

I crinkled my nose up and shook my head with a sour face. "No. Just no," I said.

"Your friend is right. Though the color is fun on you, that one is not right for you. You need something with more shape to it."

I tried on my first couple of dresses and didn't find any to my liking. My last gown to try on was nice, but the fabric was a bit heavy. Personally, I didn't like how high the neckline went up on it, but the plumb-colored silky fabric caught the light in a pretty way, which Jewel and Glen both remarked on as well.

"I definitely like the darker colors on you. But something just doesn't add up. I'm missing something with you," Glen noted.

"I like the shimmer, and when you use your power there, I think it will look really nice," Jewel mentioned.

"Wait. Wait just a flying minute. What about

this power of yours?" Glen asked.

"Oh, it's just so neat!" Jewel raved. "Esmari here is going to be a presenter at the festival this year. Like in front of everyone. And her power is just so amazing. Well, both of her powers are cool. Because she has more than one, you see—"

"Jewel—"

Jewel continued, "And she's been asked to put together a presentation with her power for the festival. She hasn't decided what she will be doing with her power just yet. But whatever it is, it's just going to be awesome. You see one of her powers is Mind Sight, and she's a Sage as well. A Sage uses this form of Energy—Sage Energy stuff—kinda hard to explain—and it makes her wings—well that's kinda hard to explain too—but it looks cool. So, anyway, she's a True Sage. Which is probably why they asked her to present. So much cooler than my power, that's for sure—"

I sighed and looked at Glen with embarrassment.

"Does she do this a lot?" Glen whispered.

"The rambling? Yeah, this is normal for her," I noted.

"—I'm really excited to be going with a

presenter to this thing. So, we simply must look our best. Es, you should do that thing, so your wings fill out. That way Glen can see what I'm talking about. And so he doesn't think I'm just some lunatic or something."

I chuckled under my breath for a moment as I looked at her hopeful eyes. Swiftly, I flicked a spark of power onto my fingertip and watched as it flickered through the different pastel colors freely. The power seeped by way of my veins and through my wings, as they filled out to their true shape.

I relished the release of pressure within me, allowing my tension to melt away once more. The moment of relaxation was more evident each time I used my power, and I was finding more and more how in tune I can be with the world around me.

Glen's eyes glittered with adoration. I could see his mind soaking it all in and considering possibilities. With a simple twirl of his finger, he silently asked me to rotate. A slight gasp left his lips as he saw the entirety of my wings.

"Well, now this changes everything, beautiful!" Glen exclaimed. "A fabric like this just won't do. Much too constricting. What *you* need is some tulle, or organza, maybe. Something to simply glimmer with you. I have a couple of pieces, but nothing in your size at the moment. Like I said, never got my stock today."

I smiled. "That's okay, I think I need a break anyway."

"As for you, Jewel—" Glen started. A tingle crept up my neck as the door to the shop opened.

"You know, I don't know why you insist on going to these Central District boutiques for your dress. My family's personal designer could just make one for you," Belleza's unmistakable voice echoed into the shop.

"I just saw one passing by here earlier that I want to try on," Lilly said. "It was this really pretty red color."

I glanced at Jewel, standing in the ruby red dress. Her eyes widened. *You have got to be kidding me. Maybe it's a different red dress?* I watched as both Belleza and Lilly's eyes rested on the dress Jewel now wore. *Of course, it's this one.*

"That one? That's the dress? Well, it definitely will look a whole lot better on you than it does on her." Belleza smirked. "I certainly hope *that* is not the dress you are planning on wearing, Esmari. Though, I'm not too sure any dress will help, well, you."

I sighed. Glen glanced at me for a moment.

"Come on, Jewels. Change out of that, so that Lilly can try it on. Oh, and excuse me, you must be the attendant? Can you please set my friend up in a fitting room? Esmari, you seem finished with yours. We can just use that one. We are meeting someone for dinner, so we are just here for the one dress," Belleza demanded, shifting her weight.

Glen stuck his hand on his hips and cocked his head toward me. I could see him take a breath and consider his next move carefully.

"Come on, you weren't going to buy it, were you Jewels?" Lilly asked.

"I mean, I don't know—" Jewel said, looking down at the fabric floating around her.

"Jewel, we all know you look awful in it. Okay? So, just go change out of it. Maybe Esmari can be useful and productive for once, and she can help. We don't have all day," Belleza scoffed.

"Okay, nope!" Glen sassed, raising a hand and pointing at the door. "Out. Get out."

"You can't just tell us to leave. We are paying customers. What is your name?" Belleza asked.

"Glen. And being that this is *my* shop, I

absolutely can ask you to leave. So, bu-bye!" he sassed right back.

Belleza huffed and Lilly rolled her eyes arrogantly. They gathered themselves and exited the shop. Glen shook his head and tossed his hands on his hips.

"Honestly! I cannot believe the audacity sometimes." Glen sighed. "Some people think that if they have parents in important roles and some cash, they can act any way they want."

"Yeah! Wait—" Jewel started. "Do you know who that is?"

"Belleza, if I'm not mistaken. And the designer her family has is a good friend. After today, I guarantee that they will be looking for a new designer. I already had someone else interested in hiring her, so it will be a perfect trade-off," Glen schemed, his voice trailing off in thought.

Jewel and I looked at each other and giggled. She swished back and forth in the dress once more and looked it over in the mirror.

"Maybe, Belleza was right about it though. It's definitely not great on me," Jewel said sticking her nose up.

"Oh flutters, the color is atrocious on you, It

makes you look mad and clashes with your hair. But the dress itself is not terrible," Glen noted, poking at some of the fabric. "If it was something more like this—and your color is definitely in the blues—oh! I've got to make a quick call. You ladies change and come meet me up front when you're done."

Jewel and I exchanged a look of confusion, but who were we to argue? We gathered ourselves and I snagged my shoes to put on. For a moment, I released a surge of power from my toes and could see Glen happily on the phone. He chatted away with a glinting of passion in his eyes.

Coming back to reality, I placed my feet in my shoes, quickly lacing them, and linked arms with a confident Jewel. Glen replaced the phone on the receiver just as we joined him.

"Okay, so I think I found the perfect dress for you, Jewel, but it's not in my shop. It's in the shop up the road. Now, she's already closed for the day, but I just got off the phone with her and she will hold it for you. So go ahead and swing by sometime this week to give it a try. It has everything you liked from each of the dresses and in a color that will complement you nicely, I do believe," Glen praised. "You are going to look stunning!"

Jewel gleamed with excitement.

six

By the end of the week, Jewel and I had still not had a chance to go together to the store holding the dress for Jewel. She seemed to have plenty of opportunities to go on her own, but she refused to go without me, saying that it just wouldn't be the same experience. So, we had agreed to go later that afternoon, which left me with extra time on my hands once again for my studies.

Mr. Sean had dismissed me early that day, due

to a meeting of some sort. I didn't ask questions, but he didn't seem all too happy about going. I decided after a long while in the classroom to take my studies to the outside grounds. It was a beautiful day, and it felt like a complete waste to stay indoors.

I wandered out of the classroom, making sure to close the door all the way today, which had been not wanting to latch, lately. Mr. Sean said that someone would be fixing it soon, though I'm not too sure how true that was. He's been saying a lot of things.

Once outside, I decided to go around to the open field, at the back of the academy. A slight breeze brushed my bare ankles where I had my jeans rolled up. I found a level area in the field, far enough away from the academy that I wouldn't disturb any classrooms by being a distraction.

The pinching at the nape of my neck was familiar and unwelcome at such an abrupt intensity. I sat down on the ground and got comfortable, not entirely knowing how long I would be there. The one thing I was aware of, was that with each passing moment, it was more evident that I was about to see none other than Byrein. Carefully lacing my hand in the grass, I closed my eyes and allowed the warmth around me to fade away.

Just as expected, Byrein came into view. His crow-like, black feathered wings shone in the sunlight coming through the nearby trees. He stood tall and confident as he peered forward.

Slowly, the rest of his surroundings came into view. A man sat with his back facing him. He nodded to Byrein. His thirsty smile curved at the corners of his lips. This time I couldn't tell if he was aware of my presence yet.

Byrein lifted two fingers and placed them just below the man's shoulder blade. He breathed in a satisfied breath, and I could feel as he released a small surge of power.

Someone came up beside him. The person stepped softly. They were blurred to me, but I could tell the person was a woman.

"Are you getting things in order?" Byrein asked in a trance.

"Yes, things are coming together nicely," said the woman. Her voice had a hint of disdain so subtle that it came across as arrogance.

"Good. Good. Things need to be absolutely perfect for when she comes and joins us," Byrein half-whispered

"Are you sure that she'll come this time?" asked the woman.

She. Are they talking about me?

He took a sharp breath, and I noticed the woman take a step back.

"I'm sorry, I don't mean to doubt. I just hate to see you disappointed," the woman soothed.

"She *will* come this time." Byrein's voice became more agitated. He pulled away from the man abruptly and I heard a small gasp slip from Byrein's lips. "Look what you made me do!"

"I—"

He ran his hand through his hair and took a breath. "No, no. It's alright. It wasn't really working anyway. His power was resisting the manipulation. Which doesn't help. But thank you, sir, for your sacrifice of time and power."

Byrein patted his shoulder with one hand, and with the other, he pressed two fingers against his shoulder blade once more. The man became ridged for a moment and then slumped over, as if his very purpose had been fulfilled and he was now at peace.

"Would you mind?" Byrein asked, motioning the woman to the man.

"Of course. I'll take care of it," the woman said

confidently. "I always do."

I watched Byrein for a moment more. His eyes were thirstier than before, greedier. He was tense though, running on adrenaline. I could feel his obsession for power, for me. Thoughts of having me with him, by his side, were written all over his face. His lips curled into that awful smile of his once more, before he faded from view.

I heard my surroundings rush back into my ears and I allowed my eyes to fall closed as I reached for the stones on my necklace. The grass around me blowing in the now cool breeze. The distant sound of crickets somewhere nearby. And a very quiet breath…

Opening my eyes, I caught sight of subtle movement just to the right of me. A boy, just a few years younger than me, peered back, silently crouched. He hugged his knees with his tan arms. His dark brown eyes studied me as a puff of air tossed his messy, unstyled dark curls on the top of his head.

"Hello," I offered.

"Hi," he returned. His voice was quiet but confident.

"What are you doing here?" I asked.

"What are you?" he responded.

Fair point. "I was—uh—practicing my power," I explained.

"I do that out here too, sometimes. Though mine doesn't make me like you were. You know," he looked around, *"vulnerable."*

I chuckled. *Another fair point.* "What's your name?"

"Omar."

"Well, Omar, were you sitting over here to watch over me?" I asked.

He nodded.

"Thank you. I'm—" I started.

"Esmari. I know you," Omar moved a smile to his lips.

A chilly breeze sent a shiver down my spine, and I glanced at Omar, who sat unfazed in his tank top, shorts, and sandals. He looked ready to spend a day at the beach.

"Cold? Here," Omar offered. He rubbed his hands together and blew gently at them, sending a warm puff of air to surround me. "Heat. It's my thing."

"Thanks. That's really neat," I noted.

"Terrible in the summer," he stated blandly.

I nodded. *I could see that.*

"Well, time to go!" Omar commented quickly. Before I could say another word, he stood up and silently sprinted out of sight into the trees.

I stood for a moment and stretched, thinking about Omar and his odd behavior. Though, he was kind and I found myself grateful for him. I gathered myself and headed to the front of the academy, where I found Mr. Higgens strolling the front pathway. I nodded a friendly hello as he approached me.

"Ah, Esmari. Hello, child. How are studies?" he asked, his deep voice echoing off the pavement.

"They are going well," I noted.

"And how are preparations going for your presentation at the festival? Have you thought of what you will do for your presentation?" he asked. Somehow, I knew that question was coming.

"I'm still giving it some thought," I answered. I could see his forehead lines deepen as he frowned slightly.

"Well, I do hope you figure it out sooner, rather than later. That festival will be here before we know it!" He chuckled heartily.

An anxious smile spread across my lips.

"Esmari!" Jewel's boisterous voice called out. "There you are! Are you ready to go?"

"Headed out for the day?" Mr. Higgens prodded.

"I am picking out my gown for the festival today, sir!" Jewel announced.

Mr Higgens smiled. "Glad to see one of you is preparing for things." He nodded goodbye and was on his way back into the academy.

"What was that about?" Jewel inquired.

"He was asking about my presentation." I sighed, his backhanded words still stinging in my ears.

"Oh! So, you figured something out?" she asked excitedly.

I frowned. "No." I watched the excitement falter in her eyes.

"Well, that's okay, I'm sure you will figure out something." Jewel linked arms with me and tugged at me. "Come on! I want to see this dress!"

We shortly arrived at the shop where Glen had the dress held for Jewel. I don't know if it was because Jewel was rambling on about something that happened in class, or if my mind was still wandering, trying to figure out what I would do for my presentation, but the journey to the far end of Central District did not seem as long today.

Jewel was nearly bouncing as we entered the shop. The fresh scent of lilacs and clean linens wafted our way. A woman with a loose bun of red hair and a face of freckles greeted us gracefully.

"Hello," she said, pressing her black plastic framed glasses into place.

"Hi! My name is Jewel. Glen sent us. He said you had a dress on hold for me," Jewel stated confidently.

"Yes! I've been expecting you." She waved us over to where the fitting rooms were located. "Please wait here while I retrieve your gown, miss."

Jewel leaned over to me with a smirk on her face. "I feel so posh, you know, requesting a dress on hold."

"You sounded very official and important," I giggled back.

The woman came around the corner with a beautiful sky blue-colored satin gown. Jewel's eyes glinted with satisfaction in the color. She took the gown and disappeared behind the cream-colored curtain of the fitting room.

"Oh! Es! It's so pretty. Flutters! It's so pretty!"

Jewel called. She flung the curtain open with pure excitement.

The gown draped beautifully over one shoulder. The shine of the dress nearly matched her wings and their own shimmer. I watched as she moved and revealed a small slit up one side that reached just above her knee. Carefully she fluffed the bottom of the dress, and we watched it fall around her.

"Es! Isn't it just perfect!" Jewel squealed.

"I love it on you, Jewel," I confirmed.

She continued with a joyful look spreading across her lips, "And wait. The best part is—"She shoved her hands at the sides of the dress, and I watched her hands disappear within the fabric. "It has *pockets!*"

I giggled with her. "That is truly made for you."

"I take it that we will be purchasing this dress?" the woman commented.

"Oh, yes. This is the perfect gown for me," Jewel stated with a confident nod.

A prickle ran across my skin as I allowed my gaze to land on the window at the front of the store. Just for a moment, I thought I saw a glimpse of the odd man from the coffee shop. *Es, you're probably just allowing your imagination to get the best of you.* I smirked to myself and took a breath.

Jewel and the woman were discussing hair options and accessories. I decided to wander about the store and glance through the gowns they had on display. This store noticeably had fewer gowns than others around, but it was probably just because of the upcoming event that they were being all bought out.

I looked at some shoe options she had and even brought a pair of heels over to Jewel, to try on with her dress, but they didn't seem to fit her well. The sun began to set, and I started to realize just how tired I was from the long week. Thankfully, Jewel nodded to me to go relax outside for a bit while she finished up.

I yawned as I stepped outside. The evening breeze was picking up and it felt like a spring storm was rolling in. And here I was, unprepared for the cool evening in a plain t-shirt and jeans. I hugged my arms tight to my chest and soaked in the evening sky, watching as it became a deeper shade of orange.

"Here," said a familiar voice behind me. I turned to see Kasius holding out a jacket my way.

"No, it's okay, Jewel will be done soon," I

protested.

He shook his head with a smirk and slung the jacket over my shoulders. I felt the chill melt from my bare arms. The inside was warm, like it had just been worn.

"Thanks." I sighed. "Kasius—"

"You know where to find me," he called over his shoulder, as he stretched his wings out. With a fluid movement, he lifted into the sky.

"I leave you alone for one minute and you already have some guy's jacket on?" Jewel scoffed playfully.

"It belongs to Kasius," I said, rolling my eyes at her.

"Uh-huh," she said, eyeing me.

"What?"

"It just—well—you look good in his jacket." She smiled and opened her wings.

I sighed and allowed myself to smile. A leaf on the ledge of the store window caught my eye as the breeze flipped it over. The once-waxy leaf looked brown and dried up on the other side.

I attempted to steal another glance, just as a gust blew the leaf out of sight. I shook my head, rubbing my tired eyes. Glancing at Jewel already in the sky,

I opened my wings and followed her home to the dorms.

seven

A whistle from the wind against my dorm window caused me to wince. It reminded me of the awful sound of ringing in my ears that I would sometimes get after a Sight episode. I placed the cap on my pen and glanced over my letter, for my family back home.

I thought of Bray's face when he read of my dislike in the windy weather today. How he would probably roll his eyes and wonder if I was telling the truth. I wondered if it was windy back home in Athra.

Dad would be happy just to hear from me, or at least that's what they always say in the letters. I thought of Mom's glittering eyes as I told her about shopping with Jewel, leaving out the presentation part, of course. *I bet her next letter will say something about how I should wear my hair up. She always did like it when my hair was up.*

I slid the letter into an envelope and addressed it to home, before standing and gathering myself for the day ahead. Kasius' jacket resting at the foot of my bed caught my eye. I hadn't seen him around for nearly a week now and felt like I had unintentionally kept his jacket hostage. With a sigh, I tossed it over my arm and decided to leave it on his door.

It was quiet in the dorms today. Most everyone was probably out and about, already starting with their day. I didn't have a set time for lessons with Mr. Sean, so, leisurely going about my morning, I wasn't in any rush to go anywhere today.

Once in the hall, I headed toward Kasius' dorm room and listened to the way the wind howled against the building, not at all eager to go outside in it just yet. It was ominous the way that the howling echoed through the empty halls. The sound of my own shoes against the floor, as I took each step, didn't help much either.

As I passed the sitting area, a figure caught me off guard. They were slouched more than normal, but I knew just who they were. Kasius sat with his hand resting across his forehead, and his book gripped loosely in his other hand strewn over the arm of the chair. His eyes were closed as he faced mostly away from where I stood.

"Kasius?" I said softly, hoping not to startle him.

Immediately, he dropped his hand and sat up straight. He opened his eyes and looked at me with what I could only describe as the most fake, gentle smile on his lips. The kind of smile you give to be polite. But I could tell something was off and bothering him still.

"Hello, Esmari," he said.

"I haven't seen you lately," I started. I held out the jacket toward him. "I wanted to return your jacket. I was just going to hang it on your door for you, whenever you got back."

He nodded and went to stand, before drawing a short, sharp breath. His eyes widened ever so minutely, and he promptly settled back down in the chair. He looked dizzy from exhaustion but didn't want me to know. I watched as he brushed his brow with his fingertip and shook his head slightly, before returning his face to the polite fake smile.

"You can just leave it there, I'll take it when I get up," he offered.

I nodded and draped the jacket on the nearby chair. I paused for a moment and pressed my lips together. "Are you okay?" I asked, hesitantly. "It's just—I haven't seen you in days and you look exhausted—"

He nodded with a sigh. "Just tired. I went home to visit Gran. She wasn't feeling well, so I went to take care of her."

"Oh! Well, how is Jan now?" I asked. The thought of the boisterous, always-on-the-go, woman feeling unwell and needing some help made me somber. She was in such high spirits all the time when she graciously allowed me to stay with her this past winter. It was almost difficult to imagine her not that way.

"She's doing better. She says hello, by the way." Kasius chuckled gently.

I smiled. "That's good to hear. Tell her I say

hello as well, and I hope she feels back to her regular ol' self soon."

Kasius nodded. We sat in silence for a moment longer. I could see his eyes drooping from pure exhaustion. *This isn't like you.*

"Well—" I paused, looking him over once more. Finally, I raised the letter still residing between my fingers. "I should get this down to the outgoing mail bin."

Kasius nodded slowly.

"You should get some rest," I offered gently.

I turned awkwardly and walked off, silently hoping he would take my advice.

As I descended the echoing staircase, the lights flickered for a moment, as if we were about to have a power outage. I didn't expect one here, for some reason. Back home in Athra, sure. We would have them quite often in the storms, but here in Banshui? I don't know why, but it just seemed odd. Maybe it was because I still have it in my head that where Royals reside, nothing like that could happen. In my brain, Royals with their incredible powers still prevent that.

I chuckled to myself at how silly that concept now sounded, being a Royal and all. Smoothing the seal of the envelope one last time, I placed it in the outgoing mail bin. A gust of wind blew into the entryway of the dorms as a familiar face entered the building.

"Hello, Esmari!" Corbin greeted cheerily. His long black hair looked tangled from the wind as it lay in the ponytail down his back. He adjusted the mail carrier on his shoulder and smiled.

"What are you doing here?" I asked. "And with a mailbag, at that?"

Corbin chuckled. "Well, Maya and I are heading out to some towns as a favor for Agathin. We are joining a friend who usually delivers the letters, like yours, so I thought I'd give him a hand in collecting them, too."

"That's nice of you! Will you be delivering mine? How are they? My family I mean," I inquired, hopeful for any information from back home.

"Yes, I certainly will if I can. I don't normally frequent the same towns much; it draws too much attention, as I'm sure you can imagine. But if it gives me an excuse to snag one of your mom's baked goodies, then I will try. I'll let you know how they are when I am back," Corbin noted sympathetically. He lifted a kind hand and gave my shoulder a pat.

"I thought Maya, well Royals in general, don't go to towns often," I pondered aloud.

"She doesn't. They don't. Maya is a Pathfinder though, remember? She sometimes is asked to help with the travels, you know, making the portals to get from one place to the next. She won't be entering the town, just helping to get there," Corbin explained.

That makes sense, I suppose. "Well, be safe," I smiled.

Corbin nodded, and I stepped past him toward the door. I tugged my sweatshirt's muted green sleeves down and prepared myself for the weather outside.

As I traveled to the academy, I allowed my brain to wander on what my presentation would be for the upcoming festival. It was better than thinking about the wind whipping my hair around on my back, creating mounds of tangles for me to work through with my brush when I got home later. A shadow floated across the pathway in front of me, as someone attempted to fly in the gusty winds.

I felt at a complete loss regarding my presentation. I wasn't sure what they wanted to see from me, but now, knowing I was presenting alongside Belleza, the pressure was starting to get to me. I felt torn. Most of all I felt insignificant. *Belleza, on the other hand, probably already has a spectacular presentation planned out. Knowing her it's going to be grand and scripted and well-rehearsed.*

I let out a sigh and opened the large heavy doors to the academy, nearly stumbling in as another gust of wind pressed at my back. I smoothed the stray strands of hair. The commotion in the entryway was surprising to my ears. I wasn't used to being at this part of the academy this late in the day.

"Es!" called Jewel, pushing her way past a group of girls. "Oh hey! Es!"

I smiled at my friend's franticness. "Hi, Jewel."

"Hey, I know we planned on hanging out this afternoon, but I've actually got to fly out. My teacher wants me to head over to a nearby medical office today to start some observations. I'm sorry, I know we had plans. Can we postpone?" Jewel rambled sheepishly.

"Yes, that's fine." I smiled. I was disappointed, but what was I supposed to say? No? "Good luck!"

Jewel gave me a rushed hug. "Thanks, Es!" Before I could blink, she was out the door.

I made my way through the groups of chatting students and walked to the classroom, not sure what

I was going to focus on today with my study time. Part of me hoped that Mr. Sean would give me another one of his tasks or have a book he wanted me to read through and reflect on.

Part of me just wanted to focus on my own studies, because I didn't understand what the purpose was of some of the assignments that he had for me lately. Mostly, I think I was just hoping for some sort of inspiration to plan for my presentation.

The classroom was just as quiet as usual, and messy too. Mr. Sean started to reorganize some of the library books last week, and it was clear he didn't finish as he had planned this morning. I closed the door with as little sound as possible and meandered into the room before me.

I glanced down the way toward the door of Mr. Sean's office, which remained propped open, but didn't hear a sound, nor did I feel the presence of his power. *Mr. Sean must have stepped out.*

A pressure at the nape of my neck caused a dull ache to spread into my shoulders as my Mind Sight beckoned. *Now's as good a time as any. Might as well take advantage of the time you have the classroom to yourself, Es.* I sat on the ground, brushing a few grains of sand away from me on the dusty brick flooring.

Taking a deep breath, and stretching my neck one last time, I released a surge of power from the pad of my fingertip. This time, though, I didn't allow it to take me just anywhere. I focused on a path. I wanted to know where I was going. I wanted to see how I got to where I was in this episode. And, this time, I found that I didn't feel drawn to anyone. Specifically, I didn't feel drawn to Byrein for once.

I watched as the halls blurred past me. I was still in the academy, rushing past doorway after doorway, until finally entering a classroom clear on the other side of the building. I allowed my focus to fall on someone with long brown curls, knowing immediately that I was looking in on Belleza, alongside a whole group of students, as well as an instructor.

I watched as she went to a large basin of water. She placed a hand just above it and strained her fingers. The water became still, as if I were looking at a piece of glass. With a smooth, sharp movement, she forced her hand upward, pulling the water up into the air in a stream.

Her other hand came into play as she began to form the water into an intricate design. She played with the liquid as if it were a string, pulling and looping until she had the design she was satisfied with.

I lurked among the group, listening to them gasp in admiration. She pushed the design higher into space above her, lifting it high into the air for all her onlookers to see. The light beaming in from the window glistened through her design, giving it a new life.

I slipped back into reality. I pulled my knees to my chest. My fingers found the charms on my necklace, and I sat for a moment thinking of the power I just saw from Belleza. It was, dare I say, spectacular. Dazzling even. And sure to wow a crowd. No doubt, it's at least part of her presentation at the festival. And here I sit, inching closer with each day to this festival, which I am meant to present at, with not a single idea in the world.

I allowed my face to fall into my knees as I grunted into the echoing space around me. Mr. Higgens' words ran through my head. *"Plus, they requested Esmari — by name." What exactly did they want to see from me? What is it that I can do that will be interesting to watch?*

I felt as though I no longer wanted to present.

Maybe Mr. Sean was right, maybe it was a bad idea. Or maybe I just don't have what it takes to present. I don't have a flashy ability.

More so, I am not exactly one who can turn heads like Belleza can with her mere presence. She can walk onto the stage and look like she belongs. Then she will wow the audience with her abilities. I mean, sure, I am getting more and more control over my abilities, but I feel like my Mind Sight is what I have the most control over, which is not exactly something I can display.

A swift knock on the door startled me, I looked up to see Mr. Higgens entering the classroom. He glanced around at the mess of books on the ground and shook his head. He smoothed his mustache with two fingers just as his gaze landed on me.

"Oh, hello, child," Mr. Higgens greeted. "I was looking for Mr. Sean."

"I think he stepped out. I'm not too sure when he will be back," I offered with an apologetic smile.

"That's quite alright. I personally think he has been avoiding me these days," Mr. Higgens noted with a chuckle. "How are preparations coming?"

"For the festival?" I asked, secretly hoping he was implying something else entirely.

"Yes, of course for the festival! I just saw Belleza. She is one of the other presenters from the academy this year. It seems that things are coming together nicely on her end," Mr. Higgens boasted, shifting his weight on his cane.

It took everything in me not to have a snarky remark. "Well—" I started. "Does she know I am also a presenter?"

"Well, come to think of it, I'm not sure. She sounded as if she already knew who else it was. I didn't think to tell her myself. Though the way she was talking, it didn't sound like you. Maybe, I should clear things up," Mr. Higgens thought aloud.

"No, no—uh—I mean—it's okay. It might be better if she doesn't know. Not many people seem to know that it's me, and I'd like to keep it that way for now. It would be a nice—uh—surprise," I stammered.

"Well, child, it sounds like you must have something up your sleeve! Don't tell me a thing about it! I want to be surprised along with all the others!" Mr. Higgens proclaimed, stamping his cane down, just missing his toes. "I will let you get back to your preparations. The festival will be here before we know it!"

I forced a smile. *Yeah, and I think that at the rate I am preparing for this grand thing, I will be surprising myself as well.*

Mr. Higgens exited the room, and I was left once again to my own thoughts. I decided to close my eyes and just be for a moment. The presence of his power faded further and further away. I felt as the doorknob he had just held lingered with reminiscence of his energy and the office on the far end of the classroom lingered with Mr. Sean's energy.

I flicked a spark of power to my fingertip and watched the light seep into the darkness behind my eyelids. I allowed the power to fill all the cracks and emptiness of my wings. They flowed with power, licking the floor at the very edges. The feeling of the flow of tension leaving my body was invigorating. It cleared my head.

Carefully, I opened my eyes and flicked another spark on my opposite hand. I allowed the power to grow, to engulf my hands. I watched the colors flicker between my fingers. I thought of the beautiful blue sky on a clear day and watched the sparks fade to the color.

The power spread up to my wrists, my

forearms, my elbows. Slowly, I pressed my hands closer and closer together. I wanted to connect the power with the other. To create one entity.

A bead of sweat dripped from my face, but I didn't care. No matter how hard I forced, my hands would not meet. Suddenly, my arms grew tired and flung apart, sending sparks raining down around me. I listened to the sizzle, as they snuffed themselves out on the cool brick around me. One spark caught the drip of sweat on the ground below me, and I watched as it flashed with a bright glittering light, just before it disappeared.

Standing up, I looked around to see what mess I would need to clean up before Mr. Sean got back. A few piles of books nearby had toppled into the walkway, and I had knocked the podium completely over from the force of the power separation, spreading a pile of loose papers across the floor. *Nice one, Es.* Reluctantly, I got to work on putting things back to how they were.

BANG!

The door swung open and in scurried Mr. Sean, making me nearly jump out of my wings. He looked almost as startled as me to find someone here. His eyes darted around, and he kicked the door shut with the heel of his boot. His hand held a paper clutched inside a fist, wrinkled from the wind.

"You're here! Good, you're here," he said in a raspy voice. Mr. Sean looked as if he hadn't slept in days. "What are you doing?"

I looked at the stack of papers I had been collecting from around the toppled podium, not sure how to answer.

"Never mind. Leave that. Come with me!" he demanded frantically.

eight

I followed Mr. Sean, not daring to ask what he had in mind, or where we were headed. Out of the classroom, and through the halls, all the way out of the academy.

To my dismay, it was still very windy outside, and I frowned as some dust blew into my eye. I rubbed at it frantically, to clear my vision. We passed Mr. Higgens somewhere along the way, who looked just as confused as I was.

We finally stopped out in the field behind the school, and I looked around at the nearby bushes and trees bending in the gusts. I attempted to pull my ponytail tighter on my head but could still feel the loose strands of hair tossing around and brushing against my ears.

Mr. Sean shoved the paper in his pocket and turned to me, searching my face, and searching his brain for his next sentence. It was something in that moment, which made me see his relation to Byrein. Something about his eyes.

"Okay, okay. So, I want you to try touchin' my power again," Mr. Sean instructed.

"Mr. Sean—"

"You need to know how to control it. You need to work on that," Mr. Sean insisted. "Remember how you paused my power? See how quickly you can get to my power and pause it."

"I—" I could tell there was no protesting this time. "Okay."

He turned his shoulder to me and waited. I took a breath and reached out two fingers, pressing them just below the shoulder. I released a surge of power and felt as it rushed toward his power's source.

I pulled further and further away from the

sensation of the wind on my face, as I felt myself drawn to his power. How it radiated through his body, and his eyes. With a quick pinch, I paused his power, as if cutting off its airway. I could feel it pressing against mine. Swiftly I released and pulled away, not wanting to allow for the craving to kick in.

His lip curled as he turned to look at me. "Good. Good. That was your fastest time yet. Smooth and controlled," Mr. Sean stated.

He pulled the paper from his pocket and fought a gust of wind to glance over the penciled notes scratched across it. Satisfied, he pushed the paper back into his pocket once more. I could feel a presence watching us, maybe two. As Mr. Sean thought, I looked around us and caught eyes with Mr. Higgens observing from afar.

"Let's do it again, but this time I need you to try activatin' your Sage power before. I need you to be a True Sage when you try this time. So, maybe if you activate it, or whatever it is you do, before tryin' and then touchin' my power, let's see where that leads us," Mr. Sean said.

"I don't know, Mr. Sean—" I started. The idea seemed wild and unsafe. "What's the point of doing that?"

"This might be the link of your powers. Let's find out," Mr. Sean lured. He turned his shoulder to me once again.

"Mr. Sean, I really don't think this is a good idea," I protested. He didn't seem to be even listening to me anymore. I glanced at Mr. Higgens who had made his way closer to us.

"Maybe—and if—this—then if it works—" Mr. Sean muttered.

I turned to Mr. Higgens. "Mr. Higgens? I really don't know about this."

"When you're ready, Esmari," Mr. Sean called over his shoulder.

Mr. Higgens held a serious face as he spoke. "It's alright, child. Mr. Sean is offering himself for the lesson, he's either aware or going to be aware very soon of the risks involved."

This didn't feel like a lesson to help me. It seemed odd. Something in me knew that the purpose was not to help me find the link between my powers. Something in me was telling me that there was another purpose Mr. Sean had in mind. That I was an experiment to solve some sort of problem.

I looked once again at Mr. Higgens, and he gave a slight nod to me from where he now stood just a few feet away. It was as if he knew that this was a bad idea too but couldn't stop the madness. He looked prepared for the worst.

I took a breath and stepped up to Mr. Sean. I tried to block out the surroundings. The sound of the wind in my ears growing more and more aggravating as my stress and tension rose. *This is ridiculous.*

I flicked a spark at my fingertip and felt as it danced around with the gusts of air. I waited as I sensed my wings fill out to their fullest behind me. They cut into the gusts of wind. Carefully, I raised two fingers up to Mr. Sean's shoulder, not aware of what to expect this time around. I resented the feeling of uncertainty now riddling my bones.

I closed my eyes and released a surge of power. Instantly, I was at the source of his power. This time it was different, though. This time, it looked different. It was a creamy, off-white color and vibrant, like a lightbulb. I could feel every molecule of his power as it pulsed, seeping closer and closer to my touch.

As Mr. Sean closed his eyes, the power grew

calmer, almost dormant, less prominent. I reached out for it. For its core, just as Mr. Sean opened his eyes once again. The intensity of his power was like a rush which I didn't want to end for me. I fought that feeling with every fiber of my being. I could feel his pain, his anguish. And I wanted to stop it for him.

Just as I had in the past, I pinched it off at the source. I could feel him relax, his tension lesson. But I could feel something else. Something more intense. An electricity. And it was coming from me. I could feel it seeping closer and closer to his power. It was like an electric snake, slithering through my veins.

I held it back as best as I could. Holding his power, pinching it off, was also allowing for my Sage Energy to not creep any closer. I knew I would eventually have to let go, but I was terrified that I wouldn't be able to let go and recoil fast enough.

I could feel my muscles shaking, growing weak from the strain I was putting them through. I had to make it quick. I listened to my own heartbeat, now pounding in my ears. Along with sneering, thirsty words.

Let it happen.

Byrein's voice echoed, sending a shooting pain

through my head. I flinched, feeling my Sage Energy creep closer yet to Mr. Sean's Sight power's core. I didn't have any other choice but to pull away; and pull away *fast*.

It terrified me.

*Okay, Es, you've got to do this. Three... two... one...*I yanked my hand away as swiftly as I could, feeling the disconnect happen, but not before a spark of Sage Energy flickered from my finger.

As if the world slowed down, I watched everything around me fade back into view. Mr. Sean, just a foot in front of me, stumbled forward. He looked bewildered, placing a hand on his head.

I took a step back, and then another, as if I were falling so slowly that I didn't understand what else to do. My body felt like static. For that matter, so did my brain. A gust of wind knocked me off my feet, and I watched Mr. Sean and I go crashing to the ground.

Then, it was all dark.

———

Opening my eyes, I felt groggy and confused. There were bright lights above me and a scratchy wool blanket covered me. I moved my hands and toes, then my arms.

A cool tube of some sort brushed against my skin, and I wanted more than anything to take the tape off that was keeping this tube in. It was itchy and pulling at a single piece of hair on my arm.

I tried to think back on where I was. How I got here. What I was doing here. I remembered the wide-open field. I remembered Byrein's voice. I remembered the feeling of Mr. Sean's power at my fingertips. It all came rushing back as I relived the memory.

"Es!" Jewel's voice rang.

"Jewel," I greeted halfway as a whisper.

"Now I know I said we were postponing our evening together, but that didn't mean you had to demand my attention like this!" Jewel teased. I could tell she was nervously trying to lighten the mood. "But, really? What did that crazy old teacher have you trying today that would send you guys to the medical clinics?"

"Mr. Sean! Is he okay? I—he—well I didn't— you see, he had me trying—I didn't mean to—" I stammered, sitting up on the hard mattress. Why were words so hard?

"Woah. Okay. Hey, it's okay, Es. I'm going to go let Mr. Higgens know you are awake. Just, um, try to relax," Jewel said. She jumped up and scurried out of the room.

I looked around at the walls plastered with this dark beige wallpaper decorated with an odd, splotchy, lighter beige pattern. This, of course, was complemented by a single matted picture of some waves, or at least I think that's what the artist was going for.

The floors were a tan ultra-glossy tile which didn't quite match the walls. And then in the corner, was a single brown leather chair. It was as if they were trying to make the room look classy, but I just thought it looked hideous and bland.

A knock on the door sounded. I glanced over to see Finn strolling in, his shoes squeaking against the clean flooring. It was odd to see him in the maroon scrubs and name tag pinned to his pocket.

"Es?" Finn's eyes lit up, then became sympathetic when he caught sight of me hooked up to the tubes. "What are you doing here?"

"I think a lesson didn't go as planned," I noted. "What are you doing here? You look official."

"Yeah, well. I am a Room Attendant right now.

Basically, I check in on patients and let the nurses and docs know if they are needed. I take care of all the little stuff, new blankets, snacks, water, finding remotes, cleaning up stuff. But it's just while I learn more about the medical field," Finn explained.

"That's neat." I smiled.

"Yeah, so I was just making my rounds to the rooms I am assigned to. I just started my shift, so I have to go and introduce myself to everyone and check in," Finn noted. He straightened his shoulders and cleared his throat. "So—hi, I'm Finn, I'm a Room Attendant here at the medical infirmary center. Is there anything you need?"

"No, thank you, uh, Finn was it?" I smiled and shook my head. That was a mistake. My hand flew up and clamped my neck, as a surge of pain radiated up through my head and down to the tip of my left wing.

"Woah, take it easy there, Es. I'll have some painkillers sent over along with the doctor to check on you," Finn cooed calmly, stepping forward to my bedside. *He certainly fits this job.*

Finn turned and left the room. Not more than a couple of minutes later, Jewel returned with Mr. Higgens. He looked calm, which I took as a good sign.

"It's good to see that you're awake, you took a nasty spill there. How do you feel?" Mr. Higgens asked.

You encouraged me to try the ludicrous idea in the first place. I tried to keep my temper under control. "I'm okay. Just sore mainly. My wing kind of hurts."

"Yes, well, from the looks of it, you landed pretty hard, but nothing is broken though," he noted.

"And Mr. Sean?" I asked sheepishly. I was terrified of the answer to come.

"Sean is fine, child. Going to be a bit sore I would suspect." Mr. Higgens adjusted his cane before he continued. "But he is going to rest here for a few days. His body is exhausted, and, flutters me, we could all see that he was sleep deprived. Something was bound to give. His desperation and hyper-fixation on the lesson were evident, I'm just sorry to have had to ask that of you. I assumed it wouldn't have the best of outcomes, but I also had hoped it wouldn't have affected you in that way."

"I'm just glad he will be okay," I half-whispered.

"Please know this was not your fault. Both Mr.

Sean, as well as I, asked this of you. But I must ask, do you know why he was so adamant on this—on your abilities in this way?" Mr. Higgens inquired.

So, he suspects something more then, too. I thought for a moment, not wanting to say something that would make Mr. Higgens think anything wrong of Mr. Sean. Sure, I was suspecting something too, but I could tell that there was tension between the two men most days. Anyone spending more than a minute with them could tell that.

"He just is trying his best to prepare me and help me understand my powers in the only ways he can. He's not a Mind Sight, so the lessons can be trial and error at times," I stated. "No two powers are *exactly* the same, I'm sure you know that better than anyone, sir. So sometimes, lessons need to be a bit off the wall to get somewhere."

I could see Jewel eyeing me slightly from where she stood behind Mr. Higgens' view. I looked away, hoping she wouldn't add anything to the conversation. To my surprise, she kept her lips sealed. Though, it looked like she was doing so with great difficulty.

"Esmari, child, I also wanted to ask something else. Do you remember much about what happened? The reason I ask is your wings became a solid color for a few moments. It was this off-white, cream-like color, and then they began sending small flickers of sparks off, somewhat like what happens with your Sage Energy. But, well, in a stuttering way. You flinched, and it was as if something had disrupted you, just before you and Mr. Sean disconnected, you see," Mr. Higgens pondered. "So, I wonder if you remember what had disrupted you, maybe so we could prevent that in the future for you, child. I just want to know how to help."

Byrein's voice echoed in my head, and I knew just what he was talking about. I looked at Mr. Higgens. He seemed innocent in his questions, and his eyes looked at me sorrowfully.

But behind the sorrow, I sensed something off. I couldn't tell why, nor what it was, but something in me just didn't want to bring Byrein into the conversation. Something made me not trust Mr. Higgens. At least not for this.

"No, sir, I'm sorry. I just remember the cream color. It was so vibrant. Everything else is still fuzzy," I lied. A blatant and utter lie. To the Head of the Academy. It was something that he maybe didn't need to know. The Byrein part at least. And thankfully, he seemed to buy it.

A swift knock on the doorway saved me from further explanation, as well as the questioning look now being flashed at me by Jewel. Mr. Higgens seemed fooled, but not my dear, inquisitive friend.

A woman entered and explained to me that she was a doctor and that she would be checking my vitals. She adjusted the tube, which she called the "IV," and made sure that the bag it was hooked to had plenty of fluid. She looked over my neck and my wing, pulling and poking, which I didn't care for.

Apparently, I had a pinched nerve in my neck that was causing the pain all the way to the tip of my wing. She gave me something that was supposed to ease the pain but seemed concerned about some swelling.

"Alright, well, I'd like to keep you here for observation overnight. If everything checks out in the morning, then you can be on your way. If you need anything at all, please let your room attendant know." She smiled politely, and with a nod, she left the room.

"Well, you get some rest, Esmari. Maybe take a day or two off from studies," Mr. Higgens noted with a stamp of his cane.

"I'll bring you something comfy to sleep in and be back in maybe an hour?" Jewel offered.

I handed over my dorm key and watched as they both left the room, leaving me inevitably to my swirling thoughts.

nine

Jewel had stayed with me the entire night, though I'm positive that she got more sleep than I did. I found myself tossing and turning all night long. However, I'm not sure if it was because the bed was so uncomfortable, or if it was because I couldn't find a position to sleep in that wasn't painful for my shoulder or my wing.

The thoughts running through my head constantly weren't helping though, either. Thoughts of Mr. Sean. Thoughts of Byrein. Thoughts of the craving my veins had to connect my power to Mr. Sean's, and Byrein's coaxing to do so. I wondered if he knew what would happen, had I really allowed my Sage power to merge with Mr. Sean's Sight power.

Finn came to check on me a few times through the night, though I pretended to be asleep most of the time so I wouldn't bother him, and so he could attend to others who likely needed something more than I did.

By late morning, I had been released to go home, with the warning that I needed to take it easy for a few days. No flying, no classes, no experiments with power. As nice as that sounded, we passed at least a dozen stores on the walk back to the dorms, all of which had front window displays advertising the upcoming festival, which I still felt at a complete loss for presenting at.

The weather today was at least nice for our walk, unlike the nasty wind from yesterday, which gave a little bit of peace. The sky was a pretty shade of blue again, completely rid of the dust that tainted it yesterday, I noticed, as we rounded the corner of the pathway. I could see the dorms up ahead, but I could also see a very snarky-looking Belleza, and what was worse was that she could see me.

Belleza turned to Lilly and flicked her perfectly groomed eyebrows at her with a smirk spread across her lips. Kasius and another male student I saw on occasion at their lunch table followed just a few steps behind. Kasius seemed significantly more himself today than he did yesterday. Well rested, and stone-faced once more.

Jewel's rambling about some story she was telling stopped at the sight of their posse. I don't know what the story was exactly about this time, but it seemed far more interesting than being in the situation I knew I couldn't avoid with Belleza.

"Did you hear, Lilly? Some student from the academy put an instructor in the infirmary yesterday," Belleza gawked.

Lilly played along, eyeing me. "Oh, dear, Lezzy! I wonder what class they belong to," she commented mockingly.

"Oh, it was that one student from the Sight class. I think she even put herself in the infirmary too," Belleza noted smugly. "I just simply couldn't imagine not having enough control over myself and my powers like that. How would my instructor ever trust me again?"

"Oh, I just don't know!" Lilly squealed.

Belleza reached back and snatched Kasius' hand in hers. "It's a good thing that Mr. Higgens made the right choice in the presenters for the festival coming up in a few short weeks. Otherwise, we all might be in danger."

Kasius eyed me quizzically, and then Belleza. He studied her face for a moment. Swiftly, he slipped his hand out from her grip and continued his way past her, and ultimately past Jewel and me. Belleza pranced forward and caught his elbow with her delicate hand, and the others followed at their heels.

Seeing her hold onto him like that boiled my blood in a way I couldn't describe. It was like she was claiming him for her own, and without his permission at that.

I looked at Jewel, who was now red hot with anger. She didn't know what to say at first. She turned to shout something back at Belleza, but by the time she figured out what to say, they were out of sight.

I sighed, ultimately not having the energy to engage in any part of the matter. Not with Belleza or

Lilly. Not with Kasius. And not with Jewel.

"Just forget it." I sighed. "Why don't you tell me more about whatever it was you were talking about before? Something to do with your shoes, or was it your hair?"

Jewel let out a big, annoyed huff. "You weren't even listening before, were you!"

"I—"

"Wait—what was I talking about before?" Jewel asked, perplexed. Her hand sat on her hips, and she tilted her head back and forth, trying to think back. "Oh, that ridiculous, annoying, pompous Belleza! She just gets me so worked up that I can't even remember what I was talking about. And what's that about her comment? That they picked right for the presenters? Does she still not know that *you* are one of them?"

"Nope. And you are not going to tell her," I insisted. I tugged at her elbow to continue our way to the dorms.

"Fine," Jewel frowned disappointedly. She turned to me thoughtfully. "Then I take it that you haven't gone for your fitting?"

"For my dress? No, you know that. I haven't found my dress yet. And what would that have to do with Belleza?"

"No, not your dress fitting. Have they not scheduled you yet?" Jewel said, giddiness filling her eyes, the way it does when she knows something I don't.

I chuckled. "What fitting? Scheduled what, Jewel?"

"Well, I guess I'm just surprised that no one has told you or scheduled you yet. Though, I honestly have never been in your shoes, you know, as an important figure of the festival and all—" Jewel teased. I could tell she was prolonging the conversation. To my frustration, Jewel was extraordinarily good at that.

I stamped my foot down like a child throwing a tantrum. "Jewelei, formally of West District of Banshui! I demand you tell me at once what you are talking about. You are keeping information from me, and I insist on knowing at once!" I stuck my head up snootily and cracked a smile.

"Okay, okay, don't get your wings all tangled," Jewel giggled. She linked arms with me and pulled me into the doorway of the dorms. "From what I heard, the officials—the ones in charge of putting the festival on, that is—bring the presenters to the

Ruling family's crown forger. And the presenters have crowns custom made that they are obligated to wear to the festival. It's a way of showing that they are supposed to be there, and they are of importance. You know, set you apart from the crowd."

"Yeah, right." I rolled my eyes at her. "Ha, ha. Very funny."

"No, I'm serious! Es, it's so cool! They always look so pretty and elegant," Jewel said, walking backwards up the stairs.

"This is a joke, right? First, I have to dress up in a big fancy ball gown, with the shoes and the hair, now you're telling me I have to wear a crown. What's next?" I said in disbelief. "Jewel, will you please turn yourself around? You are going to fall walking backwards like that. We just came from the infirmary, and I really, *really* don't want to go back."

Jewel grunted and turned back forward to climb the rest of the stairs. "Fine."

"Thank you. And I'm still not buying it," I muttered.

"Well, I've obviously never presented. But I do know it's a thing. My mom had a friend who presented at The Regal Festival years and years ago.

That's what happened for them. All the presenters were brought in together and fitted for their custom-designed crowns and tiaras," Jewel explained. She handed my key to me. "So, Belleza will have to know you are presenting with her, one way or another."

I tried to imagine the surprise on her face when she finally finds out that I was the other presenter for the festival. Though, I was a bit nervous that she would try to sabotage me and my presentation. *Would she really go that far though, Es? I mean at such an important event. Even Belleza isn't that crazy.*

"You just go in and relax some, Es. But mark my words. You will have a crown on your head when you present!" Jewel sang, gently pushing me toward my door. "I'm going to freshen up, maybe take a shower. Let me know if you need me. I'll check on you in a bit before I swing by the academy for my afternoon lab."

I entered my dorm and closed the door behind me, finding warmth and comfort in the space before me. Nothing like the boring infirmary room I had spent the night in. I felt relaxed in my private space, though my walls could use another decoration, or two.

Compared to the infirmary room I stayed in, my dorm was designer, but compared to Jewel's dorm, my dorm was plain. I smiled to myself, thinking of all the bright colors in her space, in contrast to the muted tones of my room.

I glanced at my bed, practically calling my name, and rubbed at my still-sore neck. Kicking off my shoes at the foot of my bed, I soaked in the cool floor against the pads of my feet. Carefully, I lowered myself onto the bed and allowed myself to drift off into slumber.

A rhythmic tapping on my door sounded what felt like only minutes after I closed my eyes. I rubbed my hands across my face and sat up.

"Yeah?" I croaked.

"It's me, Jewel, you need anything?" she asked through the door.

"No, no, I'm good. Just resting," I managed to say.

"Okay, well, I'm going to the academy. I won't be too long. I'll bring us back some dinner. Anything sound good?" she offered.

"Maybe a sandwich?" I commented.

"Done! See you in a little bit," Jewel called.

I looked over at the clock, which read just past

three. *That was a quick couple of hours. If you sleep more now, you might be up all night, Es.* I took a long sigh and forced myself to retreat from the comfort of my bedsheets.

With a firm hand, I tried to massage the knot in my neck that was where the pinched nerve was stemming from, just like the nurse had shown me before I left the infirmary this morning. It helped a little.

They had warned me when I left, about using my powers as well. How I needed to be careful and cautious, or not use them at all. I understood the risk, and possible prolonged soreness to go with, but I also understood something else.

The alternative risk. The risk of not using my powers.

Thankfully, the Sage in me lay dormant for the time being. My Mind Sight, on other hand, was becoming increasingly more prominent, being that I hadn't released it since yesterday. This time, it was a feeling of being called. It's like that feeling you sometimes get when you just know someone is talking about you. And I knew just who it was that was talking about me. *Okay, Byrein. Let's see what it is you are up to.*

I sat on the ground, with my bed propping up my back, such a familiar spot for me on days that I knew the episode would be on the longer side. I allowed my comforter, draped over the edge, to pad my wings as I got nice and comfortable. A release of power, and I was whisked away to the land of the Exes. The home of Byrein.

He came into view, and it was evident that he didn't know I was there. We were inside a tent, lit by flickering torches. His wings flicked as he spoke, and I could see his eyes glinting with greedy desire.

"Things must be perfect for when she arrives," Byrein instructed. "How are the preparations going?"

A woman, who I couldn't quite see correctly, stepped forward. She seemed familiar from her stance. Someone I had seen before in a Sight episode. "I am preparing her tent for you now. Just as you asked."

"Good. Good. Make sure Esmari has everything she may need to be comfortable. I'm trusting you with this. This needs to feel like her home," Byrein stated.

"Yes. I have it set up, just as you instructed. Near yours. The furniture is inside, and I will be decorating it based on your instructions. We are working on arranging for additional clothing, based on the information you provided, so that she will be comfortable in what you have for her. She will not have a single thing to worry about when she arrives," the woman noted.

"Make sure that everyone is aware of where she stands with us. She is to be my partner. No one, and I mean *no one,* is to treat her as any less." Byrein sneered. His black feathered wings flicked once again on his back.

"Yes, sir."

I watched as she walked from view, leaving Byrein and me alone. I studied him. His strong posture. His eyes thirsty for power and glistening at hope. Hope of me. Entranced by the very thought that I would be joining him soon. How soon was he talking about? I didn't think I wanted to know.

"Esmari, you'll come with me this time. And you'll see that you belong here. By my side. This is where you should have been since the very start," he breathed, his voice fading further and further away, as I was pulled from my Sight episode and back to where I sat on my dorm room floor.

As my hand met my necklace, I relaxed my

mind as best I could. I glanced up and met the eyes of Jewel, who had positioned herself right in front of me, just like she had so many times before, so I wouldn't be startled. Her eyes searched mine, and I knew she was looking for answers of where I went this time. I kept my face calm.

"You're not supposed to be using your powers," she sassed.

"You and I both know that's not something that works for me," I commented softly, glancing out the window at the setting sun.

She sighed. "You were there a while. Everything okay?"

I knew what she was implying. I knew she wanted me to tell her if I had seen Byrein in my episode. It was no use worrying her about him again, though.

"Yeah. I just needed to release some power, you know? And I wanted to see the waves on the beach," I lied.

She nodded. I didn't like lying to her. I didn't usually just look for a place in my Mind Sight episodes, I usually had to see a person. A detail in which I hoped she would overlook. Thankfully, her hunger got the best of her, as we both listened to her stomach erupt with a loud growl.

Jewel let out a chuckle. "I guess it's time to eat! Oh, and you will never guess who I ran into on the way back!"

Jewel handed me a sandwich and was sent into one of her long-winded stories. I happily ate my dinner, providing a "really?" or "huh," every so often.

I watched as her eyes would light up when she talked, often using her hands to explain details. Unfortunately, she would often also forget that she had food in her hands and fling crumbs this way and that. She would sheepishly clean the crumbs up and then continue her tale.

Just as she was finishing up, my phone rang. Carefully, I stood, stretching out my half-numb legs. I reached over and snatched the phone off the receiver.

"Hello?"

"Hello, I am calling for a Ms. Esmari?" said the woman on the opposite end of the line. Her voice held an accent which made her seem prim and proper.

"Speaking," I responded.

"Ah, Ms. Esmari. I was told I could reach you

here. I am a coordinator for The Regal Festival. I am calling to schedule you for a fitting. I am told you may not know many of our traditions, but as a presenter at our upcoming event, the Ruling Family would like to fit you for a custom-made crown or tiara. This is something we ask that you wear during the duration of the festival but is yours to keep. Our fitter has set aside time tomorrow afternoon at two o'clock for our presenters. I have already cleared this with Mr. Higgens at the academy so that it won't interfere with any studies. If you could just meet me outside of the academy at one-thirty, I will escort you and the other presenter from the academy to the fitting."

I turned to Jewel, wide-eyed. "One-thirty tomorrow. Thank you! I will meet you there."

"Thank you, Ms. Esmari. Goodbye," she said and hung up.

I looked at the now silent phone sitting in my hand with disbelief. Replacing it to its receiver, I turned to Jewel slowly. She seemed to already know what the phone call was about, and she sat up smugly.

"Well?" she asked arrogantly.

"You were right," I said with a long, overly

dramatic sigh.

ten

As I walked toward the academy, I found myself adjusting my shirt over and over, nervously. I had tried on about a dozen outfits for today and couldn't find one that was just right.

It seemed silly, but these people were people who worked with Royals. I mean not just Royals, but *the Ruling Family* of Royals. The top of the top when it comes to Royals. And here I was, a dirt head. Someone without Royal parents. Someone of little significance, who didn't even know this place existed a year ago. I at least wanted to be presentable.

I don't own many fancy clothes and was kicking myself for always choosing comfort and a good bargain over classy and expensive. *Would it have really killed you to spend extra on at least one outfit? I mean you are given a generous allowance every month for being a Royal from outside of Banshui, Es.* I shook my head and tugged at the hemming of my shirt once more.

The money I was given was supposed to help with expenses and such, being that I don't have a family to help from here. But I was always frugal with it, mainly because I didn't trust how long I would be receiving it. But also, because it still felt a little weird to spend money that was basically gifted to me, just because I moved to a new town. Jewel was always a tinge jealous, and made it sound like the allowance was for life.

A thought of Belleza popped into my head. Someone from a family of money, complete with a large mansion. She absolutely was going to be well dressed today. Classy, I'm sure, and poised. She will look like she belongs today, while I will look out of place. Like I had been invited out of pity. And I am positive she will make it evident that I was.

Once again, I looked at my attire and my anything-but-fancy manicure. I was grateful I at least had a fresh coat of polish on my nails, instead of the chipped nail polish I often sported. Though I wished it matched my outfit better. Quietly, I let out a sigh as I arrived at our meeting point.

I was early. Which is what I hoped for. I didn't want them waiting on me. It was a beautiful day today, and the air smelled sweet from the pink flowers blooming on a nearby bush.

I stretched my neck as I waited, to avoid wringing at my anxious fingers. The pain from my pinched nerve was almost non-existent today, something for which I was grateful. Smoothing my bland, blonde hair behind my ears, I released a shaky breath.

It felt odd to be waiting to get fitted for a headpiece, and a crown, nonetheless. It seemed unnecessary and made me realize even more how unprepared I was for the festival. Would they ask me what I wanted for my crown? What would I say? I hardly had time to process that I'm supposed to wear a crown, so I hadn't even considered the idea of what it would look like. Am I even a crown person? Was that a thing? Would it just look silly on my head?

A panic started to form deep in my gut as I attempted to imagine my head holding a crown. Belleza looks like someone who would wear an actual crown, I look like someone who would drop one. I couldn't believe I was about to spend the entire afternoon with her. Her looks of disapproval, her judgmental remarks. I gritted my teeth at the very thought.

Though, as the minutes went by, and the closer our meeting time came, I was beginning to feel like this was a big joke. What if no one else comes? One thing was for sure, Belleza was known for being punctual, especially when it was something important.

Here I stood, though. Alone. I fully expected her to be here just moments after me. I expected to get all the awkward conversations out of the way. The degrading comments on how they must have really pitied me. Or how they were willing to just accept anyone. I kicked at a rock on the ground and tucked my hands in my pockets.

Today is just as much for you as it is for her. I

steadied my nerves. *You were asked to be a presenter. By name, no less.* Carefully, I lifted a hand out of my pocket and flicked a small puff of Energy to my nail, watching as it sparkled like a small speck of glitter in the morning light.

They requested me, but I still have no clue what they were hoping to see. My thoughts danced along with each spark of color radiating from the tip of my nail.

"Esmari, I presume?" a woman said. Startled, I allowed my Sage Energy to fizzle out. I recognized her voice from the phone call yesterday.

"Hello," I smiled.

"Great. I am sorry for being a few minutes behind schedule, I got held up. Do forgive me for that," she noted.

"The other presenter isn't here yet," I commented.

"Oh, yes, I am aware. Not to worry though. She had something important to attend to this afternoon. We rearranged so she could have a private fitting this morning. Rather kind of you to remember, though," she stated.

The woman tucked a strand of hair, which had escaped her updo, behind her ear. She wore a sophisticated navy blouse and some charcoal gray slacks. I watched as she adjusted her weight in her pointy-toed heels.

No, Belleza. One less thing to worry about. I smiled to myself and could feel a bit of tension drip from my shoulders.

"Alright, my name is Dee. Please follow me, Esmari." She fluttered up into the sky with her pure silver wings that shone in the light.

As gracefully as possible, I followed her lead, far into the North District of Banshui, thankful that pesky pinched nerve wasn't going to give me any trouble flying today. The last thing I wanted to do was explain *that* entire ordeal to this Royal Festival Coordinator.

The memories came flooding back as we passed the outdoor market I had spent so much time in when I stayed with Jan. I glanced down at the alleyway where the book shop was, where I found out about being a True Sage, and I wondered if the old man was there today.

The rooftops below were now clear of snow and ice since the wintertime, and I noticed more greenery in the plants along the ground. It seemed like an entirely different area from what I once explored. I watched as Dee veered toward another group of stores suspended in the sky.

We landed at the door of a small, insignificant-looking store sandwiched between two much larger stores, each with grand front window displays. This one just had a door. I watched as she glanced at a wooden clock sitting in the window display of the store to the right.

"It's about time you showed up!" called a man. He stepped forward, slipping his circular sunglasses off his face. A woman dressed in all black stood tall behind him and chuckled, her heavy eyeliner surrounded big brown eyes glowing with excitement to see a familiar face.

"Warren, hello! How are you?" Dee chuckled, embracing him in a warm hug, and then turned to embrace the woman. "And Kat, my dear. It's lovely to see you. I am so happy that you two will be presenting again this year."

Again? How many times have they presented? I looked them over. They both were several years older than I was and looked confident in being here. I smoothed the upturned hemming of my shirt down yet again, nervously.

"I'm just surprised they aren't sick of us yet!"

Kat teased, eyeing Warren.

"Oh, flitter flutter," Dee said, shaking her head.

"*Flitter flutter*," Warren mocked, as he tugged at his brown heathered vest, causing the chain of his pocket watch to click against a big round button.

Dee ticked her tongue at him and turned her attention to me. "This is Esmari. She is also going to be presenting at this year's festival as well."

I shook their hands. "Hello," I managed.

"So, they roped you into this whole fiasco, did they?" Warren laughed.

"Oh, don't you scare her off. It's a great honor to present. Even Warren knows that. It's nice to meet you, Esmari," Kat said. I watched as the earrings scaling her ears sparkled in the light.

"Well, we are already a few minutes behind schedule. I don't want to keep our fitter waiting any longer. You all can all chat inside," Dee noted. She opened the door for us, and I followed the others inside the shop.

We walked through a long skinny hall which opened to the main room of the shop. Warm lighting shined throughout the space from the rustic lighting fixtures high above our heads.

A tall statured man glanced over his magnified

glass, perching in front of him on the table. Carefully, he placed his tools down and scooted the stool back to stand and greet us. He was muscular, and something about his face reminded me a bit of my brother Bray, if Bray were about thirty years older.

"Hello," he said in a deep, even voice.

"Hello, Arthur," Dee greeted softly. "Here are the remaining presenters. Thank you again for arranging this morning."

"Sure. I will get right to it then." He turned to the three of us and looked us over with a rugged, bearded, calm expression. "Kat, let's start with you."

I watched as Kat followed Arthur to his desk. Warren tugged gently at my elbow toward some interestingly shaped chairs in the corner of the store. Carefully, I sat down, trying not to slouch back too much. I cringed internally as the leather of the chair squeaked beneath me.

Dee turned toward a clock, and after doing some calculations in her head, she glanced at Warren. "I hate to do this, but would you mind making sure Esmari is well taken care of? I need to stop by a few shops in the area and iron out a few wrinkles that have come up for this event."

Warren grinned as he relaxed back in the chair. He hooked the sunglasses on the V-neck collar of his white t-shirt and took a glance at Kat. "Dee, don't you worry, we veterans know the drill. She will be well taken care of in our hands."

Dee took a sigh and nodded to Kat. Kat nodded back reassuringly. I watched as Dee quietly left the shop. The uncomfortable tension in the air set in, as I was now left alone in a shop that I'd never been to with three people I didn't know. I felt their glances, their thoughts, their concerns. And all I could do was sit in silence, tightening the grip of my folded hands.

"So," Warren said. It was clear he wasn't one to enjoy the silence. He sat forward, intently studying me. A strand of his slicked-back chocolate brown hair fell onto his forehead. "What is that you do? What's your power?"

"Warren! Don't you think that was a bit abrupt? You can't just start a conversation with that. It's just plain rude," Kat scolded. She looked at me apologetically.

"Well, aren't you curious? Plus, we are presenters together, we are all going to figure it out sooner or later," Warren defended. He looked back at me and tapped a finger to his chin. "Wait, don't tell me. I'll take a guess. You're the water girl."

I shook my head. "No. That's Belleza. She's the one who couldn't make it."

Arthur raised his eyebrow at the mention of her name but didn't look up from his work. He was busy sketching away with a piece of graphite and a textured piece of paper. Kat looked over his shoulder as he worked.

"*Belleza*. That name sounds familiar." Warren smirked, eyeing Kat. "She wouldn't be the daughter of—"

"Warren. Watch what you say!" Kat warned. "You are sitting across from her friend."

"I don't think they are friends," Warren called out to Kat. "Though, I could be wrong. Are you actually her friend?"

"Um—I wouldn't call us *friends*—" I said cautiously.

"Called it. Not friends!" Warren blurted, throwing a hand in the air with victory.

I looked nervously at Kat and Arthur. He was studying Kat, her features. Arthur pulled out a worn metal measuring device of some sort and put it onto the top of her head. She looked relaxed. Like this was just another day, and another crown.

"So, not the water girl. Which means, you must be the Mixer. The one with multiple powers!" Warren exclaimed.

"Esmari, you can tell him to fly off whenever you want. I tell him to do so almost hourly," Kat noted, sticking a black manicured hand on her hip.

The silver rings on her fingers clanked against each other as she tapped them, watching Warren impatiently. Her style was edgy in a confident, sophisticated, "don't mess with me" kind of way. And I couldn't help but admire it.

"No, it's okay. Warren is right. I'm presenting, so you were bound to know soon enough," I commented. I turned to Warren. "I'm a True Sage. I'm a Mind Sight with Sage Energy. The winning combo supposedly."

"Well, now, would you just look at that? She just might give the two of us a run for our money, Kat!" Warren gawked. "So, have you figured out your presentation?"

I sighed. "I'm still sort of working on that."

"Eh, you'll figure it out. Don't stress about it too much. Just do what feels natural, however you are most comfortable using your power. Your powers are so rare that whatever you do will be impressive. Flutters, I don't have a plan!" Warren chuckled.

"You never have a plan," Kat scoffed.

"You don't know how you are going to present? What you are going to do when you go up in front of everyone?" I asked, completely flabbergasted.

"Arthur's ready for you, Warren," Kat said, nudging him to stand from the seat.

Warren flicked his eyebrows at me and strode over to Arthur's table.

Kat looked at me and shrugged. "No one knows what he will do until he is doing it. Not even him. He just wings it."

"And it works like a charm!" Warren said grandly. Arthur corrected Warren's head position with a firm grasp. I stifled a chuckle.

"Would you stop making Arthur's job any harder than it is?" Kat called.

"So, he really just goes with no plan?" I asked.

"Yup, every time," Kat said, crossing her legs and slouching back in the chair.

"I just like to surprise the audience!" Warren called.

"You are just too lazy to be bothered," Kat countered. She glanced at me. "But, they keep inviting him back, so I guess he's doing something that they like. Me? I prefer to be prepared."

I smiled. Prepared sounded less scary.

"But, Warren is right about one thing, focus on doing something you are already comfortable doing. You don't have to do anything big or grand for this. People would rather see you easily execute a presentation, than struggle to impress," Kat advised.

It was good advice, honestly. And it got me thinking. What was I comfortable doing? What did I do often enough that I could do it again under the pressure of a thousand sets of eyes watching me, no problem? My mind immediately went to the game Jewel and I played. *Well, it's a start.*

"So, what are you wanting to do for your crown? Are you going full crown or tiara?" Kat asked as she spun a ring on her finger. I was thankful to change the subject.

"I'm not sure. I didn't even know about any of this until yesterday. I haven't had a whole lot of time to think about it."

"Well, you could always match your dress? That's what I did last festival. I had this nice plumb-colored dress, so Arthur made this beautiful crown that had stones to match," Kat suggested with a small shrug. I saw a small smile of pride come to Arthur's face at the mention of his work.

"That would be a great idea, except I haven't even found my dress yet," I remarked. I looked down, embarrassed. Here I sat, no plan for my presentation, no idea what dress I would be wearing, but hey, I would at least have a crown, right?

"Wow, well, that's okay. I mean there's still some time. We still have, what? A couple more weeks? You should be fine. Let's start with the basics. Crown or tiara. A crown goes all the way around in a full circle and a tiara doesn't. Based on your head, I am going to guess a tiara would be better for you." Kat pondered. "Arthur?"

Arthur looked up from his sketching and glanced at me. "Tiara," he confirmed with a nod.

He looked back down and immediately continued his sketch, turning his head from side to side as he shaded.

"Great. One less thing to figure out. Now as for design, you don't have a dress to match. So, we can't fly with that idea." Kat contorted her face as she looked me over.

"What about your wings? I mean, you are going to bring those with you," Warren stated, as he came to join us. He leaned a hand on the back of Kat's chair.

Kat looked at me and then at Warren. She shrugged. "Huh. Could work. I think you did that a few years back, Warren. Or was it that other guy? What was his name?"

"No, it wasn't me, it was that young presenter years ago. He had some interesting wings, so it fit well," Warren noted. "Let's see those beauties, Esmari."

I shrugged. "Okay, yeah, sure."

Carefully, I backed away from the others. Arthur stepped out from behind his desk, using a wet towel to wipe his hands clean from the graphite he had been using. Quietly, he waited, ready to observe and create. I put my back to the others and opened my wings.

"Hey, they are kinda your style, Kat. All black." Warren chuckled softly, elbowing her.

I glanced over my shoulder at Warren. Part of me was excited to his face when I showed him what they truly become with the use of my Sage Energy. Kat smirked, she could sense that there was more and waited patiently. I flicked a small spark of Energy to the tip of my index finger's nail and watched as Warren's expression changed to pure enthrallment.

"And they got better!" Warren exclaimed.

I swiveled from side to side and watched the glinting colors flicker in the reflections of objects around me. The small statue on a display shelf, the half-finished crown on a mannequin head, even on the rim of the magnifying glass sitting at Arthur's workspace.

I glanced at Arthur and could tell his creativity was at work. His eyes glittered with inspiration. Kat saw too and allowed a smile to soften her face. She flicked a look to me of intrigue.

I slowly allowed the spark to snuff out on my fingertip as I tucked my wings back behind me. Turning around, I waited quietly for someone else to have the first word.

"Arthur? You seem satisfied," Kat noted.

He grunted happily with a nod. He turned toward his workstation and hunched over it, sketching away on the piece of paper, not even bothering to sit down.

"Satisfied? I think he is the happiest I have seen

him in years. Excited even!" Warren stated. "Flutters, I think he is intrigued, and challenged, and inspired! I mean, did you see that look on his face?"

I looked at Kat, who nudged me to go closer to Arthur. I obliged, careful not to bump Arthur as he worked. I glanced over his shoulder and listened to the way the graphite sounded on the paper.

He would spin the paper this way and that as he drew, creating intricate lines and swirls. There were holes in his design which he soon filled with different colors of drawn stones, each integrated so beautifully into his design, that they looked as if they were a part of the framework itself.

Arthur suddenly turned to me. Grabbing me gently by my shoulders, he positioned me in the light. Abruptly, he took my head and tilted it one way and then the other, studying what I could only imagine to be the shape of my very skull.

He took his measuring instrument and used it multiple different ways, measuring each angle of my head where the tiara would ultimately lay. He jotted down each of the measurements on a key that he created at the bottom of the sketch.

I watched as he walked over to a drawer set

beside his workstation. Arthur opened the first drawer and pulled out a display box holding several types of gems, crystals, and stones. He placed each of our crown mock-up drawings in front of him and began glancing between the stones and the drawings.

"Now for the real magic! When he makes the crowns," Warren whispered with awe.

I glanced at Warren's face and then back at the creator standing beside me, wide-eyed and absorbing every moment of watching Arthur's steps.

Arthur continued looking between the pages and reference gems. Every so often, he would jot another symbol down on one of the pages as a note to himself.

"You honestly think he would let you watch his work?" Kat noted with a roll of her eyes.

"He hasn't kicked us out yet, maybe if we be really, really quiet, he will let us stay and observe," Warren whispered.

Kat raised her eyebrows at him in disbelief. She took a sigh and glanced at me. She made a face to mock Warren's silliness. I snickered.

"Shhh!" Warren hushed.

"Warren, you know the drill. No one gets to see this part of the process. Please return in an hour," Arthur instructed.

"Aww!" Warren whined teasingly. Arthur shot him a look of annoyance. "Okay, okay, we are leaving!"

Kat shook her head. She reached up and gave Warren a shove. "Oh, fly off. Give Arthur some space. He needs time to make a crown big enough to fit your massive head! Thank you, Arthur. We will see you in an hour."

I turned to Arthur and nodded a quiet thank you before following the others out of the shop.

Once outside, we decided to find something to snack on nearby while we waited. I felt awkward and like a third wing with them, but as soon as Kat noticed my quiet trailing, she made it a point to walk with me, and make Warren the third wing. He didn't seem to mind.

Kat suggested a smoothie and juice shop just a few blocks away, raving about how delicious they were and how they always had specialty ingredients you can't find just anywhere.

We chatted about all sorts of things as we walked there. They told me a bit about the festival, and what I should expect. Warren talked about his childhood growing up right next to the beach in Coastal District. Kat was from just around the corner from where we were in Northern District. I talked vaguely about my hometown of Athra, telling them about my parents and brother and how different it was from Banshui.

Soon enough, we had all gotten to the juice shop Kat spoke of and ordered ourselves a drink. She was right about the multitude of ingredients, several of which were fruits I had never heard of, let alone tasted. I decided on the safe option of something called a "Merry Berry," which was mainly strawberries, blueberries, and raspberries, with a splash of almond milk.

"So, Esmari, since you aren't from Banshui, how did you get discovered? I mean who was the Royal who brought you back?" Kat asked, taking another sip of her bright green smoothie.

"It's kind of a long, bizarre story," I noted, thinking back.

"Oh, come on, we only know of the regular old stuff, you know, growing up here." Warren made a face. "Tell us your story!"

"Well, okay." *I guess we do have time to waste.*

"Athra, my hometown, threw this festival in honor of a Royal and their Accompanying visiting. Actually, come to think of it, the festival was just under a year ago! Beginning of summer. It was kind of abrupt and last minute. Classes had just finished for a summer break and I had just gotten my wings. I went to support my brother, Bray, at this wing race he had entered and noticed someone with wings like mine. Wings with the copper smear. I went after her and that's when I found out I was a Royal. Maya—"

"Wait, Maya? Like dark skin and has gold beads and charms in her long black braids? That Maya?" Kat asked.

"Yeah! That's the one! She's the Royal who whisked me away to Banshui," I confirmed.

"Wow! How neat! Maya and I went to the Academy together. We were pretty close. Still stay in touch, but don't see each other nearly as often anymore. Is she still close with—um—co—oh! What was his name?" Kat said.

"Corbin?" I offered

"Yeah! That's it. Are they still friends?" Kat asked.

"He was the Accompanying that came along. They are still close. I think he goes with her each time she is sent out on a task," I shrugged.

Warren slurped the last of his smoothie loudly. "Wait. So, did you get to bring someone with you? You know as your Accompanying, Non-Royal person?"

"Yeah." I sighed, looking at my straw.

"Well, I hope they are coming with you to the Festival! It would be awesome to meet them—" Warren exclaimed. I pressed my lips together.

"Warren—" Kat whispered. I saw her flick her head at him to get him to stop.

"What? Oh—" Warren's eyes lost their light. I didn't think that could happen. "You're that girl. It was your friend."

"His name was Hunter. And, yeah. I'm *that* girl. That Mixer," I affirmed, touching my necklace. *Hunter would have had fun, though. It always was his sort of thing.*

"I'm sorry," Kat said, placing a hand on my shoulder.

"It's okay. I had my time to process. Not having him here with me still hurts, but it's okay," I shrugged. "On that note, do you think our crowns are ready?"

Kat chuckled at my sudden change of subject,

and I appreciated the two of them being so willing to drop the topic. We cleaned up our trash and headed back to Arthur's shop.

My head danced with thoughts of the sketch Arthur had made, and I couldn't wait to see it in person. It felt silly and frivolous to be excited about a crown, but in my defense, up until a year ago, I thought all of this didn't exist. Not Banshui, not powers, not Royals, and not big ball gowns and crowns.

It was all like something out of a fairy tale. A secret land with powerful individuals living a life so grand and dressed all fancy. I couldn't help but feel at least a little excited about wearing a pretty tiara myself.

Arthur greeted us with a soft smile. He motioned us further inside and stood back, admiring his display. Three charcoal gray boxes stood at the edge of his workstation, each embossed with our names on the lid in copper metallic.

Kat and Warren immediately went to theirs and opened the lid. They admired their new pieces carefully. Kat's crown was delicate and looked like it was made of golden flower petals. The detail of the tiny flecks of rubies on each of the petals gave the illusion of veins. Warren's was simple, from what I saw of it. Silver with a design carved into it. Though he had already placed it back in the box before I could see much of the detail.

I opened the lid of my box and my breath caught in my throat at the beautiful piece before me. With a gentle touch, I ran my finger over the top of the cold metal. The white gold was so pure I was afraid to lift it.

Arthur came beside me and took the tiara gently from the box. He nodded toward a small mirror that he had mounted on the wall in the corner. I followed him and watched my reflection as he placed the crown on my head, securing it in place against my hair. He stepped back and admired the shape of the tiara, closely hugging the shape of my head.

The tiara looked like intertwined vines swirling their way around my head, with bits of uneven, multicolored pastel stones tangled within. I flicked a spark of my Energy to my fingernail and watched as my wings filled out behind me, sparking and flickering through pastel colors. The crown seemed to come to life as each of the gemstones sparkled in the light emanating from my wings.

It felt right.

"One less thing to have to worry about, Esmari. The rest will fall into place, you'll see," Kat whispered to me with a wink and a soft, reassuring squeeze of my shoulders.

One less thing. I smiled.

eleven

I found myself just opening the box for my tiara to stare at it in the quiet of my dorm every couple of days. I found it would give me the reassurance that I needed to calm my nerves as I thought about the festival and how horribly all my preparations were going.

Or rather not going, I suppose. Every time I would think I had an idea for a presentation, it either didn't work when I tried, or wouldn't be enough to show at the festival. However, looking at the tiara would just remind me of Kat. *The rest will fall into place, Esmari.*

Jewel constantly had pestered me, to let her see my tiara. But I was keeping it hidden away anytime she was near. I wanted her to be surprised, to see it as a whole ensemble, when I had my entire outfit for the festival. I think the suspense was eating her alive. And secretly, I was enjoying keeping her in suspense.

Belleza, on the other hand, had no problem showing just about anyone who had eyes. If you were anywhere near her for any given amount of time, she made sure that you knew she not only *has* a fancy crown, but that you had seen it in all its shiny glory.

"My dad said that he has never seen such a grand crown. He thinks that the fitter wanted me to look extra special," Belleza bragged, to a small group of newer students who just recently moved into the dorm. With glittering eyes, they were all gathered around her in one corner of the community lounge area.

Her eyes caught mine as I glanced at her from the other corner of the room where I was cozied up in a large lounge chair. She lifted the crown to her head smugly. I had to admit that the delicate rose gold design holding pink stones suited her colors well. Though, it looked kind of basic. Nothing all that special about it. Even a dirt head from Athra like me could see that.

"It matches well with the colors in my dress. We are to wear our crowns during the duration of the festival so that us chosen presenters can stand apart from others," Belleza explained while eyeing me, allowing an egotistical smile to form on her lips.

My tiara is better. I bit my tongue. The conversation wasn't worth it.

I turned back to the notes I was working on. Quickly, I began to jot down another couple of words. To my dismay, the green ink in my pen was beginning to run dry. It had been a recent favorite of mine, and I am truly surprised the pen lasted as long as it had.

A couple of sharp shakes, and a harsh scribble on some blank space on the corner of my paper, and it was evident that there was no hope for the pen. I switched instead to my pencil and continued my thoughts.

"As a presenter, I simply must look my absolute

best for the Regal Festival. I hear, if you still haven't gotten a dress to attend yet, it's starting to become tough to do so," Belleza warned the onlookers, flicking a smirk in my direction.

How is it that she knows I don't have anything to wear? Maybe she's just bluffing.

"I'm going to the tailor today with my mom to get my dress hemmed. It's my sister's from last festival," one girl noted.

"That's sweet. But, you don't have to worry about your looks, I suppose. All eyes will be on us presenters anyway. So, it's important for people like me to look the part. A well-dressed presenter will reflect highly on the festival's decision to invite that presenter. It shows you have taken the invite seriously. So, since you aren't presenting, no one will notice what you wear," Belleza assured.

She caught my eyes as I peeked at her over my notes again. Though she pretended to be informing these other students, I knew she was saying it just to take a jab at me. I took a sigh and redirected my attention away.

The girl shuddered, nodding to the others. "That's true. I'm glad I'm not presenting. It seems like so much pressure and responsibility."

"Oh! Kasius!" Belleza said, waiving to get his attention.

He was settling down in a large comfy chair by the window between the view of Belleza and me. Her voice didn't surprise him. He turned his body in the chair to face her.

"Yes?" he responded.

"What do you think?" Belleza asked, tilting her head from side to side, modeling the crown for him.

"It's nice," he noted politely, turning back and opening the leather-bound book in his hands.

"How about you, Kasius? Do you like yours?" Belleza called.

The lead on my pencil broke off, though I was pretty much done with my brainstorming. This was far more interesting. I tucked away the paper in my pocket, curious as to how he would respond to her. He seemed unfazed, turning the cream-colored page.

"My what?" he called over his shoulder.

"Your crown, silly Kasius," Belleza teased flirtatiously. One of the younger students giggled as Belleza made a face.

Kasius glanced up from his book. He pondered for a moment, and I could tell he was debating whether he cared enough to indulge her in the conversation. I watched as he released a breath.

"I don't have one," Kasius stated calmly.

Belleza chuckled. "All presenters have a crown. Why are you being so shy about it?"

Kasius peered out the window with his face of stone. The page pinched between his fingers twitched, as the air from the vent caught it. "I'm not presenting at the festival."

I stifled a giggle as I saw Belleza's face contort with confusion. "But I thought — Mr. Higgens said — Well, then who is it?"

Kasius shrugged and returned his gaze to his book. "Not me."

Belleza stuck her hands on her hips. "Huh."

She returned her attention to the students around her. I gathered my things and tossed them in my satchel, hoping to leave before the topic came up again.

After a quick stretch, I stood. Kasius took a sigh, and I watched his eyebrows twitch. For a moment, he flicked a glance at me.

He released a silent smirk and allowed the corner of his lips to curl. With a shake of his head in satisfaction, I could tell that he put it together. He knew I was the other presenter. *Just don't tell Belleza.*

I decided to take myself for a walk to enjoy the nice weather. As my sandals hit the path below me, I listened to the muffled noises of the world around me.

My mind wandered once again on my powers. I had been so focused on my presentation lately, that I had not taken the time to just *explore* my powers. To live them and let them breathe. I had used my Mind Sight when I needed to, or my Sage Energy when my veins hurt enough, but I had stepped away from just exploring their true nature.

I thought of my Mind Sight. The ability to control it. The ability to see further and further. I thought of how it seemed connected, always to a person, rarely just to a place. But it always had to do with a destination someone was residing in, in the moment, something they touched. It always led back to the person.

My Sage Energy fed off that electricity that I felt. That connection that everyone has with everything around them. I thought about the feeling I got when I released it. The relaxing sensation that would spread throughout my body as the tension eased inside my veins.

I wandered my way into the Academy, to the classroom. I was alone, as expected. Mr. Sean wouldn't be back until tomorrow. He was on strict orders to get some rest. To reset. Mr. Higgens explained to me that he wasn't allowed to return any sooner, in hopes that he would be a little more sane and put together.

I personally hoped for that too, but I wasn't going to hold my breath. He was probably driving himself mad with the extra time to just "relax." I don't think that word is in his vocabulary as of lately.

I strolled around the classroom looking at the bookshelves for anything that could be interesting to read. As I came upon the back bookshelves, near Mr. Sean's office, I noticed his door wide open. A dangerous, slippery slope of curiosity was getting the best of me and dragging me down. I couldn't help but just peek into his office.

It felt wrong, and I didn't want to be rude. I didn't want to snoop and find secrets. But I wanted to know what was behind the always off-limits room. The room where he would grumble to himself and shut himself in. The room where he would go to work on solving whatever it was that he was always working on to solve.

I just wanted to understand. Was that so wrong? Was that violating trust and privacy? Maybe. But I was going to anyway.

I pressed the door open just a tad further with the pads of my fingertips. An eerie creek from the ungreased hinges. Craning my neck, I peeked in. Some part of me still expected to meet eyes with an unforgiving Mr. Sean. Carefully, I released a breath and eased my tense shoulders down as I took in the sight before me.

Papers were strewn all over the floor in piles, which I am sure made sense to Mr. Sean. Some were his writing, some looked like notes from others. Some had shoeprints on them from Mr. Sean's boots, because he couldn't be bothered to step over them as he paced the office and pondered.

A rolled-up, scratchy-looking light blue blanket was tossed in the corner by an empty box for the same snack bars he always seemed to be eating. The chunks of peeling leather from a beat-up, old chair were dusting the floor.

Carefully, I stepped in, attempting to only use the open bits of brick flooring as a pathway. I didn't want to leave any shoe marks on his papers. He may not care, but I did. Honestly, I didn't even think he would notice someone else's shoe prints on the papers, but I also didn't want to risk it either.

Rotating his desk chair for a better view, I looked around at his basic wood desk. A dusty desk lamp sat at the corner, its base covered in snack bar wrappers and crumpled notes, neither of which made it to the waste bin just a foot away from the desk. A half-drunken water bottle balanced on top of a small stack of worn books at the center of the desk, each with little yellow sticky notes marking different pages.

I began to notice a theme on the torn papers littering the surface's spare space. Many were marked in the corner with his handwriting. The notes, the pages from books, even some of the hard-to-understand sketches; all had a simple question mark and my name in red ink.

I looked around where I now stood on the ground, to the piles of papers strewn about. Some had a top paper with the same, and some had a big "NO" written and circled several times out of frustration in the corner. I couldn't make sense of it. It was like a puzzle in Mr. Sean's mind, and these were the clues.

Something on the wall behind the door caught my eye. Cautiously, I tiptoed over the mess on the floor toward the door and pushed it closed. A gasp left my lips as I began to comprehend what was before my eyes.

A small brown bulletin board mounted on the wall plastered with papers sat before me. At the center, an old, creased photo of Byrein. All around it were notes of him. Of his powers. Of his capabilities. Of his tendencies. It outlined different times Mr. Sean had seen him over the years and his progression. I tried to make out what some of it said as my eyes danced around the notes. *Mind Sight... Control... Help him... Powerful... Thirst for more... Not good enough... Seeing power... Obsession... Destroying himself... Partner... Spouse... Need to save him... Manipulation... Release power... Not Ready... Take... Solution... ESMARI?*

I stared at the big bold letters spelling my name. I didn't know what to think. These notes seemed to make sense to Mr. Sean, in his mind. And I would assume that his training, and his lessons lately, are because he thinks I am a piece in this grand puzzle of his. The solution to something that has to do with Byrein.

But I didn't understand as to how. Nor did I know if I wanted to. It was hard enough to make sense of the lessons. Now to know that he had a purpose, the chaos of these lessons he was teaching me was just that much more confusing. Were the lessons because I was the solution to Byrein, or were the lessons to protect me from him?

I didn't know for certain, but I definitely felt that the lessons didn't have much to do with protecting me against Byrein. One thing was evident, though, Mr. Sean saw me as a piece in this whole conundrum and was training me as such.

Part of me now regretted exploring this little office of Mr. Sean. Maybe it was better to be in the dark about these things. To not know. To just be on the other end of the curiosity, rather than keeping quiet about knowing what I now know. Knowing I was just a pawn in his strategy game.

Then again, that feeling wasn't new. I always felt that way. It was like I was waiting for the right push. To pull just the right cards in this game. For the right sequence of moves so that I could take my turn.

In some ways, this doesn't change a thing. I still would have to tread lightly around Mr. Sean, just like I had for such a long time now. I still would be waiting on Byrein's next move. But now, if I think of myself as a piece in this, maybe, just maybe, I can play along.

And maybe it wasn't just Mr. Sean's game, or Byrein's.

Either way, this was turning into a game of strategy, and, in order to not just be a useless pawn, I needed to play my part. I needed to think strategically, anticipate Byrein's next moves, and maybe even Mr. Sean's. I needed to be one step ahead. Whether I liked it or not, I had a role in this. So, I might as well start preparing my plan of action, for if and when Byrein makes his next move.

That starts with deceiving Mr. Sean.

He needs to think, without a shadow of a doubt, that I was oblivious still to all of this. That I don't know the reason behind his chaotic lessons. And most of all, that I am still willing to try anything new he throws at me.

I took one last look at the dooming bulletin board before exiting Mr. Sean's office. I was careful to leave absolutely everything, including the creaky door, just as I found it.

I wanted fresh air. I craved it after the stuffiness

of Mr. Sean's office. It didn't seem like it, but I had spent almost an hour couped up, exploring that tiny space. I wanted a space to just think. Somewhere less quiet. A space that wasn't here, and I set out for it.

I missed the days that Jewel and I were just discovering my Mind Sight. The simplicity of our little game. Where she would form a shape with some water, and I would use Sight to see what it was. Something so simple could relieve my tension when my Mind Sight persisted. It seemed childish now. To want to play a guessing game.

I listened to a group of boys laughing in the entryway as I passed. One was telling a very animated tale from the events that happened in his class to some friends. It brought a smile to my cheeks hearing the lighthearted laughter.

I wandered the pathway outside for a moment, not sure where I was wanting to go. A cloud from above cast a shadow on the pavement in front of me as it passed. I watched it as I felt my wings spread behind me, whisking my body off to the Dripping Crown's comfortable front doorstep.

The shop was busy again today, and Victor's smiling face showed excitement for his booming business. I placed my order and found a space to sit at the bar. Carefully, I propped my satchel on the ground and waited for my drink. A slight commotion caught me off guard as a woman tripped, catching the back of my chair and bumping into someone along the way.

The skin on my arms prickled as I understood what had just happened. I found my mind yanked away from the thoughts of Mr. Sean's office. Her eyes widened with embarrassment, realizing just what happened, and began apologizing frantically.

"It's okay. It was an accident. Are you okay?" I asked.

She nodded. "Yes, yes. So very sorry, again!"

I smiled and adjusted my barstool.

Reaching down, she picked up a small flower in her hand. "Wait! Sir! You dropped this!" she called as the door opened.

I glanced over at her hand. At a small bud of a white flower, with a familiar waxy leaf perched at the stem. My mind raced.

"Can I see that?" I asked. She handed the flower to me and was on her way. There was no mistake in my mind.

Frantically I looked to the door and caught eyes with the man's familiar face. His intense look made me certain that this was the same man as before with the unusual power.

He nodded to me and closed the door. I stood from my barstool, just as the flower leaf gave a little pop sound turning the flower into a waft of smoke and dust. But just as it began to clear the air, a faint shadow of four letters appeared.

help

My heart raced inside of my chest, rattling my ribcage. I wanted to find the man. I wanted to understand. Why me? Why here? Why now? What was it that he thought I could help him with? I jolted away from the barstool behind me. Toward the door. Something in me needed to see him. To answer his plea.

"Es?" I heard Victor calling out after me, as he placed my cup where I once sat.

"Hang on. I'll be right back," I muster.

Why didn't he just talk to me? Was this his way of communicating? I didn't understand. But I wanted to.

My hand touched the cool metal handle, and I felt the muscles in my shoulder contract as I swung the door open. My eyes darted all around for any ounce of hope that I would catch the man.

I just wanted to speak to him. I didn't know how to help him, but he asked *me*. Of all people he could have asked. It was me.

What was it that he knew I could do, which others couldn't? Was it something to do with my Mind Sight? Something to do with my Sage Energy? Was it because I was a True Sage?

The man was nowhere to be found. Not even a trace of where he could have gone. I knelt and pressed a fingertip to the ground, as I had done so many times before. I launched into a Sight episode, desperate to find him.

Nothing.

It was as if he had disappeared among the shadows.

———

I found it hard to sleep most of that night. I thought a lot about the man. What he needed me for, or why he would trust me with reaching out for help. I couldn't put a finger on it.

By morning, my mind was preoccupied with

something else entirely. Mr. Sean to be exact. The guilt of snooping in his office was eating me alive. I didn't like lying to him. But then again, how long had he planned to keep the whole charade up on his end?

You just have to keep it together, Es. He doesn't need to know that you snooped, that you know anything at all. Just play dumb, he won't think anything of it, I reassured myself. Every bone in my body was telling me lying was wrong. Lying to a teacher? Very, very wrong. I was brought up better.

My brother Bray and I were always taught to be respectful and honest with everyone. That especially applied to teachers and authority. But at this point, it all was beginning to feel like a game of survival. And I didn't know who to trust.

Mr. Sean greeted me at the door of the Academy, looking surprisingly well rested. Honestly, it was the first time I had seen him freshly showered and not so haggard. He nodded toward me a polite hello, before shrugging a silent invitation to follow him to the field behind the Academy once again.

We had been spending so much time out here lately which had been a nice change of pace with the spring air. But sometimes, I just missed the privacy of the classroom to work on lessons.

We stood for a moment in the grass, and I took note of how much taller it had gotten since it was last cut. A few yellow dandelions were sprinkled throughout the field, swaying in the slight morning breeze. I took in the smell of the air surrounding us and thought of Jewel. When the air smelled sweet, like it did on days like today, one could almost count on it to be a warm afternoon.

Slowly I allowed my eyes to wander back to Mr. Sean. Carefully, he brought a hand up to his head and ran his fingers through his brown hair.

"Esmari," Mr. Sean started, searching for the right words. "I just wanted to apologize. I didn't listen to you. You know your powers better than me, that's for sure. You knew it wouldn't be a good idea. I forced you to try somethin' that was dangerous for the both of us. I allowed Mr. Higgens to talk you into it just as much. I let my judgment get clouded and it could have been much worse."

I stood flabbergasted. I didn't know how to respond to his politeness. I almost wanted him to be his grumpy self. I wasn't prepared for this.

"It's okay," I managed. "This is sort of new

territory for the both of us, you know? We are both okay now."

He nodded and pushed up the sleeves of his trench coat. "So, what would you like to work on today? Let's maybe take it slow today. For both of our sakes."

I smirked as I watched him sit on the grass. "I'm not sure," I said joining him. I laced my fingers between the blades of long soft grass and embraced the cool sensation.

"Well, have you figured out your presentation? For the festival, I mean?" Mr. Sean asked.

"You actually want to talk about the festival? I thought you were completely against me doing that," I scoffed.

"Well, you have made up your mind about doin' the thing. I am well aware that I am the last person who can change your mind about it," Mr. Sean sassed.

"Honestly at this rate, if I can't think of anything soon, I will disappoint whoever it was that requested me." I sighed.

"You haven't got a clue?" Mr. Sean pondered for a moment. "Well, what about that thing you used to always do? That game you played. You know with that water girl?"

"You mean Jewel?"

"Yeah her, you used to do that all the time," Mr. Sean noted.

"Yeah, I've thought about that too. And I mean it's a start, but it's no presentation," I stated.

"Well, you could always do something like it. Incorporate that Sage Energy of yours somehow. It doesn't have to be all that grand. Your powers are different enough, they will entertain the audience for sure. Throw a couple sparks, find some shapes, call it a day." Mr. Sean shrugged, laying back in the grass. It seemed odd to see him so relaxed. I hated to admit this kookie teacher of mine might be onto something though.

He took a large, exaggerated stretch, grunting as he did so. Carefully, he got himself up off the ground and turned from side to side.

His wings twitched and his brow furrowed. They looked worse than before. The scarring extending further into his wing than it had prior. I swallowed hard, knowing very well that it was our little experiment that caused additional damage to his already deformed wing.

I laced my fingers once more in the blades of

grass below and allowed a surge of power to release from my palm. An individual quickly came into view nearby. He stood watching us nearby a tree, unsure of how to approach.

His gaze, however, was unmistakable; that of the silent man from the coffee shop.

I blinked out of the Mind Sight episode and stood to my feet. Looking across the field, I watched as the man approached. Mr. Sean grew rigid. I could tell he was untrusting of the unusual character.

"Esmari?" Mr. Sean prompted. "A friend of yours?"

"Not sure," I whispered. "All I know is he wanted my help."

"What do you mean?" Mr. Sean prompted again.

I shrugged just as the man was within earshot. I watched Mr. Sean's jaw clench under his scruffy graying beard.

Mr. Sean glared him down. "What is it you want?"

The man didn't say anything. He pointed to his ears.

Mr. Sean stepped up, ready to block the man from me. The individual looked at me, then at Mr.

Sean. He looked frustrated and agitated. Unpredictable even. Cautiously, I watched.

"What do you want?" Mr. Sean repeated.

The man looked down at the ground. He touched it gently with the pads of his fingers and we watched as a small flower appeared. Moments later, just as with the foliage from him in the past, a small pop occurred, leaving nothing but a puff of smoke.

He took a twig in his hand which had fallen from a branch and lifted it up. Waxy leaves sprouted immediately. He positioned it away from himself, turning away, just as a string of pop noises crackled. We observed as the branch turned to dust in mere moments before our eyes.

Opening his mouth, he managed a contorted, "hewlp."

Mr. Sean's eyes softened. He pulled his hands from his pocket, allowing them to move rhythmically as he spoke. "Can you not hear?"

The man's eyes lit at the sight of Mr. Sean's moving hands. Suddenly, he was moving his hands too. *Sign language?* I had only heard of it being a language, but never had I seen it in real life.

I watched as the two of them communicated with their hands. The man was repeating some of his signs for Mr. Sean, and Mr. Sean would sign back slowly, thinking through each movement.

"What is he saying to you?" I asked cautiously.

"I'm still trying to understand. It's been a while since I've used sign language. And I am not very fluent," Mr. Sean noted, signing something back.

Suddenly, the man did a sequence with his hands and then thrust them, palms up, in my direction. Mr. Sean shook his head.

Again and again, the man did the sequence, each time thrusting his hands toward me. He let out a desperate grunt. Mr. Sean's brow furrowed once more, as he tried to grasp what the man was trying to communicate.

The man reached for a small ladybug as it landed on his shirt. I could see sorrow fill his eyes as he placed it in his hand. The ladybug fluttered gleefully, only for a moment, before landing once more in his palm.

With a pop just like before, the ladybug was nothing more than ash. We could do nothing more than watch.

He desperately signed the sequence once more, looking at Mr. Sean with tear-filled eyes, and thrust his hands toward me. Mr. Sean shook his head, this time more out of disbelief.

"What is it?" I asked.

Mr. Sean looked between us for a moment. He took a breath.

"I think he wants you to relieve him of his powers," Mr. Sean said.

twelve

"Relieve him? What? Like, take them away?" I exclaimed. I tried to wrap my head around the concept. A memory of Byrein in the forest stained my mind. I remembered how the person became rigid and then limp. My skin crawled at the very thought.

"Yes. I think that's what he wants," Mr. Sean confirmed with a subtle nod. He seemed unfazed by the idea.

It didn't surprise me that I could do that, based solely on the feeling I got when I touched Mr. Sean's power. It was fairly evident that my veins craved to allow it to seep in. Allow it to drain from Mr. Sean.

But it made me sick.

I didn't want another person's power. I didn't want to deprive them of what they were destined to be. I didn't want to know what it felt like to have their power coursing through my veins, mixing with mine.

I needed to say something. But what?

I knew I could do this. I had watched Byrein take someone's power. Being that I had Mind Sight too, it wasn't a far leap to make that conclusion for myself.

The difference is that Mr. Sean didn't know I was aware of this capability. And Mr. Sean was now asking this of me.

"You knew I could do this?" I said, emphasizing my surprise.

Mr. Sean nodded. "You can not only touch one's power, but you can manipulate it, like you did to help your friend on the beach. And you can relieve one's power."

"Won't it hurt him?" I asked cautiously.

"No. But if not in the right mindset, it could turn into an addiction for you. Based on your complete distaste in the very idea, however, I am not all too worried about that," Mr. Sean noted.

"Where does it go? When I take his power, I mean?" I asked, knowing the answer was not something I was wanting to hear.

"You take it in," Mr. Sean stated bluntly.

I knew what he meant. I didn't want him to clarify.

The man looked between the two of us. He desperately held out his hands again toward me. He took one of those hands and rubbed it in a circle on his chest, his eyes pleading as he blinked back the tears.

"He's askin' you 'please,' Esmari. You don't have to do this if you don't want to," Mr. Sean commented.

I looked again at his eyes, so full of sorrow and desperation. "He's asking for help. And knows I can help him. Mr. Sean, I think I want to help him."

Mr. Sean looked me over. Slowly, he tucked his hands into the pockets of his trench coat and nodded.

I wonder if I can just take part of it away. The part

that is unmanageable. Cautiously, I stepped up to the man and nodded. "I'll try. I can't guarantee that I can help. But I can try."

The man seemed to understand. I moved behind his shoulder, eyeing Mr. Sean with worry. Slowing my heart, I took a long steady breath, before lifting my fingers to his shoulder.

With the release of a gentle surge, I could see his power growing more and more clear. I followed it to find its core. It was different from Jewel's and Mr. Sean's. It was strange, deformed almost. It didn't seem right. Like there was a part of it that wasn't supposed to be there. The light emanating from it was intoxicating.

I reached out and touched it, feeling the rush of that familiar prickling sensation dance through me. Hesitantly, I released a small surge of my power and connected to his.

It was invigorating, yet, felt so wrong. I could see how it moved into his palms, his fingertips. I could see the potential for it to continue to the rest of his skin. Slowly the sensation seeped further and further into my fingers. And that's when I saw it.

The disconnect.

He didn't have one power. He had almost two.

Almost. It was like his body wanted him to be a Mixer, but it didn't fully form.

His dominant power was glowing. It was the one attached to his hands. But attached like a leech, poisoning his ability, was something else. Another entity of power. Like it was supposed to be a separate one.

No, not a separate one. It was like an experiment that went wrong. Like he had his power manipulated. It was that part that was unmanageable. Uncontrollable. I didn't know what it was exactly. Another power? Part of one? An extension of his dominant power? I wasn't sure. But, whatever it was, I knew that was the part that I needed to relieve him of.

I fought the urge to allow myself to crave for his power. I fought the sensation of thirst for more. I focused on the intersection of the two entities. Pinching at the attachment, I felt the energy between the two weaken.

The leach power began to struggle its way free. I knew whatever it was I was going to do, I needed to do it fast. I allowed my connection to move directly to this deformity. I felt my veins burn for it, as it seeped its way into my body. It felt like a hot sludge. *Just a little further, Esmari.*

I allowed all of it to seep into me like a toxic drug. I wanted more. I wanted all of it. Why stop there? Why not have all of it? *No. Esmari. No.* I could feel myself slipping, caving into the craving.

I wanted to pull away. I needed to pull away. I couldn't take it anymore. I released a surge to sever the tie between the power I had taken in and the power that remained, hoping it was enough.

Yanking my hand back, I stumbled over my own feet, trying to find my balance. My head was spinning. My arms felt heavy. I felt as the excess of power dissipated into my body. *I think I'm going to be sick.*

I pushed past Mr. Sean and thankfully made it to a bush in time. Mr. Sean came beside me and waited until I was finished. He handed me a napkin to clean up my face and didn't say a word.

"I think I fixed it," I said finally.

"What do you mean you fixed it?" Mr. Sean asked, confusion forming on his face.

"His power wasn't right. I think I took the part that wasn't right," I tried to explain. It sounded silly aloud.

"You mean—you managed to take *part* of his

power? Not all of it?" Mr. Sean's eyes searched my face. "You were able to control what you took? And how much?"

I nodded. My head still felt woozy. "At least I think I did," I confessed.

The man came closer. I watched as Mr. Sean tried to explain to him. He looked in awe at his hands. He knelt and pressed a finger into the grass.

We watched a tiny flower slowly grow. He plucked it off and turned it over again and again in his hands, waiting. I caught sight of the waxy leaf, so unusual on this type of small flower. The tip had a small mark of brown. My eyes glued to it, watching, waiting for it to spread.

It never did.

The man looked at me, tears spilling over his once intense eyes. He reached down and created a beautiful white flower, with the signature waxy leaf. Repeatedly, he touched his hand to his chin.

"He's telling you thank you," Mr. Sean translated calmly.

The man plucked the flower from the ground and handed it to me.

"It's beautiful." I smiled, turning to Mr. Sean. "How do I tell him that? How do I say beautiful?"

Mr. Sean tried to show me, and I attempted to sign to the man. "Beautiful."

The man smiled and corrected my hand gently, showing the sign again to me. I tried once more, and he nodded. Quietly, he turned to walk away. I could tell there was a new-found confidence in his step.

"Esmari, you did a good thing for him," Mr. Sean noted. "How do you feel?"

"Thanks. Um—I don't feel all that great, if I'm being honest, Mr. Sean. Can we call it for today?"

Mr. Sean nodded to me humbly.

I returned to my dorm room and nearly collapsed into my bed, hoping that the nauseous feeling brewing in my gut would soon subside. I wasn't like most other kids growing up. I didn't seem to get sick like they did.

When a stomach bug hit our town pretty badly, everyone in my family had it *twice*. But not me. I was fine. I just didn't get sick. Only the occasional cold, or that one time when I accidentally made a sandwich with some cheese that had been left out on the counter too long.

But, I just didn't get sick like this. So, this feeling of lasting nausea was not welcomed. Not in the least.

I felt different in a way. Not by a lot, but enough

to feel like my power was stronger inside of me. It was odd though, it almost felt more defined than before. And I'm pretty sure this new sensation of my power was what was causing the nausea.

I closed my eyes and rested for about an hour. I was grateful I did too, because when I got up, I felt much better. No spinning head, no need to run for a bush.

I snatched a carbonated water from my little dorm fridge, in hopes that it would be the refresh I needed, only to be disappointed in the flavor. Jewel had accidentally grabbed the brand that we both didn't prefer the last time she restocked the fridge. This one had a bitter aftertaste that neither of us liked.

I took a sigh and decided to take the last of them out of the fridge. I wrote a quick note on a scrap of paper and walked them down to the communal kitchen area to leave for anyone who wanted.

Glancing at the new clock hanging on a nearby wall, I took note of the time. Jewel was once again helping out at the infirmary, this time shadowing someone in the wound care department, I think. We had agreed to meet for dinner that night, however, at a little café in Central District. Being that the clock showed was only early afternoon, I still had several hours to waste.

I made my way down the stairs, and out of the dorm building. The warmth from the sun beamed down through the luscious trees shading the pathway just ahead. With a flutter of my wings, I hovered near the ground as I took in the fresh air.

I pondered on my presentation and somehow felt more at ease thinking about it. We were less than two weeks from the festival, and I felt like I should have everything planned, and figured out. My attire, my presentation, where to go, when I was set to present. Though, for as little as I had figured out, I didn't feel anxious. At least, not right now.

Something, or rather someone, caught my eye by a tree. I looked at Omar as he watched me quietly. His eyes darted around, watching me land close by. I waved to him, but he kept his hands against the trunk of the tree, softly rubbing the bark.

"Hello," I offered.

"I'm warming this tree. It seemed cold," Omar said.

I smiled with a nod.

"Did you make a mess in that bush?" Omar blurted.

"Behind the Academy there?" I clarified.

"Yeah, did you do that?" Omar asked, his head ducking.

"Uh—yeah," I said sheepishly, rubbing at the back of my neck.

"Okay. I couldn't tell if it was you or that odd teacher," Omar commented. "You are okay now?"

I smiled. "Yeah, I'm okay now."

Omar lifted his hands off the tree and touched them to the damp soil. I watched a slight mist formed at our feet.

"Bye!" Omar said abruptly with a smile. He turned and bolted in between the trees and bushes.

I shook my head. *Did he really wait here to ask if I was okay?* I watched as the mist around my ankles dissipated. It reminded me of the fog that Jewel once used to make shapes out of.

I allowed a memory of my Sage Energy dancing through the fog to play in my head. It was a memory that held so much for me. So much transition and acceptance. So much peace. I remembered the purity in the moment and how it felt to see my power used for something beautiful. A warm smile came to my lips in realization.

I was finally getting an idea for my

presentation.

thirteen

Jewel flopped lazily into the large beanbag chair beside me, handing off a small, prepackaged chocolate chip muffin. I pinched at the crinkly plastic wrapper with the crooks of my fingers and peeled it open. Careful not to spill crumbs down my shirt, I took a big bite and embraced the sweetness as it graced my tongue.

"Told you that café would be good last night!" Jewel mentioned, praising herself.

"A little pricy, and the portions could have been a bit bigger. But I admit, it was yummy," I noted, tossing the remainder of the small muffin into my mouth.

"You seem like you are starting to get excited for the Regal Festival. Does that mean you have your presentation figured out?" Jewel prodded.

"Well—"

"Right, right. You don't want to talk about it. It stresses you out. You know, as your best friend, I feel like I should know. Oh, and another thing, I should know what your crown looks like, so that I can keep an eye out for a dress for you!" Jewel eyed me.

I shook my head and glanced out at the golden glow of the morning. "I'm getting somewhere with my presentation. I think I have a good plan in mind, actually." I smiled.

"Yay!" Jewel proclaimed, throwing her hands in the air in celebration.

"And I'm not going to tell you what it is!" I sassed.

"Aw!" She pouted.

I snickered at her. "As for the crown. You don't get to see that either. But I'll give you a clue about it—"

Jewel sat up, eager for any ounce of information she could get. "Go on," she coaxed.

"It's not a crown, it's a tiara. Apparently, there is a difference," I told her.

Jewel thought for a moment, disappointment spreading across her expression. "That is quite possibly the *worst* clue!" she fussed. She released a sigh, sinking back down. "But, I suppose it's better than nothing."

"So, I never asked you. How are things going at the infirmary? You have been spending quite a bit of time there!" I inquired.

"Well—" Jewel thought for a minute. "Things are gooooing—"

"You must be doing something right, because they keep inviting you back for more!" I laughed.

"Yeah—" Jewel paused and contorted her face. She let out a massive, dramatic sigh. "Oh, Es. I—I— I hate it! It's awful! And gross! And icky! And I have no idea what is going on half of the time—and my feet always hurt from standing so much—and they seem to like me, so I keep going along with it. But it's awful. Everyone is so serious all the time. And professional—which I know makes a lot of sense for, you know, an infirmary medical place, but it's all professional talk. Even on breaks! I get that they are passionate about helping people and stuff, but it's just a lot."

"I'm sorry Jewel. What about the other day when you got to shadow Finn for a bit?" I offered.

"Yeah, I mean that was cool and all. Getting to hang out with him was really, quite nice. And I got to know him a bit more. Honestly, I think my little talks with him through the different days while I'm there, well, that is what has kept me going for so long. But, Es! They had me in wound care the other day and it was absolutely sickening. And this creepy old guy was staring at me, all googly-eyed. He kept complimenting me, all the while, he was getting this infected wound cleaned out. I just about lost my lunch. It's so much work—and so much responsibility—and things change so quickly around there—and people are mean, even when you are helping them. Don't get me wrong, people like Finn are built for that kind of stuff. But I'm not like people like Finn," Jewel rambled.

"So, quit," I suggested with a shrug.

"Yeah. I know. I just thought I had this direction, you know, for *after* the Academy. And I don't want to just be at some piping department through the town, like so many of us end up going from the Academy. I thought I maybe had this purpose for—for—I don't know—for more. My next step. Something I could make a career out of." Jewel frowned. "I was really trying to make it work. I can tell my time at the academy is coming to a close. It's time for me to take a step into the working world. I just don't know how."

I nodded. "You need to at least talk to your teacher. You shouldn't keep forcing yourself to go there, if you really don't like it."

"I know. I have an open lab in just a little bit. Maybe I can talk to my teacher about it today. Get things sorted out," Jewel noted. She stood and took a stretch.

I nodded. "Probably for the best."

Jewel took a pair of pale blue sneakers from under her bed and slipped them on. "What about you? What are you doing today?"

"Not sure. Maybe I will wander around some stores for a little bit this morning." I shrugged.

"Hoping to find your dress finally?" Jewel eyed, tugging at her pant legs.

"Maybe."

"You had better get to that. If you're not careful, there won't be any options left for you to choose from!" Jewel warned.

"Then I'll just have to be creative. Maybe I could tie my curtains into a nice skirt and wear it with a t-shirt. Should be acceptable," I joked.

"We could make that work. Maybe add a few stickers to decorate it. No one would know the difference!" Jewel added with a laugh.

I chuckled. I crawled my way out of the comfy bean bag chair and stretched my arms with a grunt.

"Could you imagine Belleza's face if I *did* show up like that? And as a fellow presenter no less!" I exclaimed.

"She still doesn't know, does she?" Jewel asked.

"No, I don't *think* she does, at least. And at this point, I plan to keep it that way," I smirked, following Jewel out of her dorm and down the stairs. Once outside, we parted ways.

It was a beautiful sunny morning today, and I felt like stretching my wings for a peaceful flutter over to the shops. I watched as some others down below were beginning their day. Some were having a chat with a friend over a morning pastry as they walked, while another couple flew by me, holding hands and planning their day ahead.

I wandered my way through a couple of shops, one we had already been to, and one that didn't seem to have much other than shoes. Neither of which had decent gowns left over. I found my way to another shop and didn't like what I had found there either.

I was beginning to grow nervous that I had waited too long. *You should have just settled for one when you shopped with Jewel. Then you wouldn't be scraping the bottom with these options, Es.*

The more stores I looked through, the more I was becoming discouraged. Though I did find a store that had a decent selection of accessories, which I took a mental note of for later.

Several shopkeepers looked at me with pity when they realized what it was that I was in their store for. It seemed almost everyone who was going to this festival already had their gown or suit, and they were just coming out shopping for their last-minute additions.

After a couple of hours, I was exhausted and left without much hope. I took a sip of the bottled tea I had purchased at a little convenience store and strolled along the sidewalk.

Most dresses I was coming across were in some odd color like highlighter yellow, which made me look sickly, or they were something uncomfortable because of the random amounts of attachments on it, like poky feathers or weird appliques. Either way, they were not for me.

Finishing off the last of the bottled tea, I tossed it in a nearby trash can and took a sigh, glancing up at the fluffy clouds high above in the beautiful blue Banshui sky.

Belleza's words popped in my head. *A well-dressed presenter will reflect highly on the festival's decision to invite that presenter.* Releasing a tense breath, and an unintentional, irritated grunt, I looked around. I decided to take a chance at another shop, not even bothering to look at the name of the shop, let alone their window display.

The shop was familiar, then again, most shops were starting to seem the same at this point. It wasn't until a familiar face popped up from behind the counter, with a roll of receipt paper in hand, that I realized where I had ended up.

Glen smiled brightly back at me with eager eyes. "Oh! The presenter! Jewel, was it?"

"Actually, Jewel is my friend," I noted.

"Ah yes, right, Jewel, powder blue satin dress from my friend up the road. You are Es — E —" Glen pondered, as he clasped the receipt paper in place.

"Esmari. And I'm surprised you remember us!" I praised.

"Esmari. That's right!" Glen noted. "Out shopping for some accessories?"

"A gown. I still haven't had luck finding, well, anything, really," I sighed.

Glen smiled slyly. "You don't say."

"Don't tell me you have something! I would be grateful if it was any color other than a shade of yellow. Or bright orange for that matter. That's all I can seem to find at the last couple of shops. I'm desperate for anything, Glen. And as Belleza has so kindly reminded me lately, all eyes will be on the presenters. So, showing up in something that looks like a mustard bottle exploded on me is going to make me look like a joke!" I pleaded.

"Ohhh, that Belleza. Well, love. It's not yellow. And it just might be perfect for you. I had a designer drop off an extra dress, just this morning. I put it in the back," Glen explained, a glint of satisfaction flickering in his eyes.

"I don't care if it is perfect, I just am looking for

something. *Anything* will be better than my current options," I groaned. *That curtain we joked about using was starting to become a very serious option.*

Glen disappeared into the storage room of his shop. "Well, I didn't want to display it for just anyone. I set it aside because a gown like this needs someone special to wear it. Honestly, it is some of this designer's best work yet!" he called.

A sliver of hope fluttered inside my chest as I waited for Glen to return from the back storage with the gown. I didn't care what it looked like. I trusted Glen, and his opinion. I trusted that he knew better than I did what would look good on me. He hadn't led Jewel and me astray before, so I just knew he wouldn't now.

Glen emerged and I felt the world slow down as I took in the spectacular gown now hanging from his arm. Carefully, he hung the silver hanger on the end of a sparse clothing rack and fluffed the bottom of the gown.

The gorgeous, deep, emerald-green fabric lay in an A-line cut, with a glittering organza overlay, which reminded me of the stars in the night sky, or of the moon flickering on the water in the ocean. The bottom was full of shape, like a true ball gown.

Attached by thin spaghetti straps over the shoulders, the top was cut into a perfect V-neck, not too deep. Elegant. Classy.

Gingerly, I touched the fabric with my fingertips, afraid to ruin its beauty. I allowed myself to release a breath, one I didn't even realize had been trapped in my throat. It was simply the most magnificent gown I had ever laid eyes on.

"What do you think? How about you try it on, love?" Glen offered softly.

He set me up inside a dressing room and I changed into the grand garment. I took extra care not to wrinkle it while I did so. A quick zip up the back and I opened the door of the fitting room. Glen gasped, clasping his hands over his mouth. Gleefully, he led me over to the full-length mirror.

"There you are, love. There's that beautiful presenter," he whispered.

I allowed a soft smile to spread across my lips. Admiring my reflection, I swayed back and forth, watching the gown float around me. Small flecks of glitter sparkled on the fabric as it settled in the gentle lighting. It was as if the gown was made for me, with my measurements. Perfect for the features of my figure. No alteration required.

"Now, for accessories!" Glen clapped his hands with excitement.

"The necklace stays, but I am open to some earrings," I suggested with a shrug.

"Fine, but at least let me clean up that chain for you, love. It could use a good shine!" he insisted, extending his hand.

I gently unclasped the necklace and handed it to him. He slid the charms off and placed them back in my hands for safekeeping while he soaked the chain.

Momentarily, he disappeared around the corner. When he returned, he had a display of earrings in one hand and my sparkling chain in the other. I replaced my necklace charms and reclasped it around my neck.

"How are you wanting to wear your hair? Up or down?" Glen noted.

I thought about my mom and a gentle smile came to my lips. "Up. My mom always liked it up."

"Oh, that's sweet," Glen smiled. "Okay, here. Let me just clip it up with this claw clip—aaaaand there! Not perfect, but it will do. As for earrings, I'm thinking one of these."

I looked over the display rack he held in his

hands. "I'm not really sure, they are all pretty."

Glen looked me over and then the earrings. "Not the studs. Let's go with something that dangles. Now, do we go with a gold? Or with a silver?"

"My crown is white gold. So maybe not a yellow gold," I suggested.

"Ah! Yes, I forgot we would be matching another accessory. Yellow gold, out. For that matter, my coppers, bronzes, rose golds, and pewter, also out." Glen separated the pieces by sliding them out of the way. "I think these could do the trick."

He pulled a pair of long, delicate silver earrings from the display and set the rest aside. Peering over my shoulder in the mirror, he held them up to my ears. Tilting his head back and forth, he finally nodded with admiration.

"You look radiant, love," Glen sighed. "And based off the way the handsome gentleman paused by the window just a moment ago, I am not the only one who thinks so."

I blushed. Quickly, I glanced at the now empty window, wondering who it was.

"You will be the most beautiful person there, inside and out. Even better, that stuck-up Belleza will be jealous. She won't know what to think of you when you present," Glen praised, giddy with excitement.

I sighed. "She's presenting too."

Glen raised his eyebrow. "From the look on your face, it seems she isn't aware that you are."

I shook my head and smiled sheepishly with a shrug.

"Oh, hun. I thought pulling my designer friend was payback for her distasteful attitude. But, allowing her to treat you and your friend the way she does, while leading her astray about your presenting. That's a whole new level of methodical revenge! It's simply savage!" Glen exclaimed.

"I wouldn't say I 'led her astray' exactly. I just allowed her to make her own assumptions and didn't correct them." I smirked. "Plus, sometimes, she's not worth the energy."

"Wow! I knew I liked you. But this! This is just brilliant. I cannot *wait* to see the look on little miss sassy pants' face when she sees you go on stage to show us your stuff!" Glen squealed.

I laughed. "Me too, honestly."

"A revenge like this, simply must be done in heels!" Glen announced. With a wave of his hand, he disappeared into the back to gather some options.

———

I admired my entire ensemble pieced together that night in my room. I watched as the golden light from my lamp glinted off the glitter on my gown's organza.

The earrings that Glen picked out complimented my crown so well, one would have thought they were made by the same person. My shoes were going to take a little getting used to, being that I didn't often prance around in heels like Belleza always did, but I had to admit, they were rather comfortable. And as Glen reminded me, I do have wings. If I am having a hard time standing or walking in them, I can always flutter my wings a little and take the ease off my feet.

A moment of peace washed over me as I started to see the pieces for this festival fall into place. So much of my time had been revolving around planning or worrying about how it would all come together. But now, I had an outfit that was fit for a presenter. And, better yet, I had an idea of a plan for a presentation.

I glanced at the note from Dee left for me with my mail, along with a letter from mom. Mom's letter outlined some things happening in town. She told me of how my old teacher Mr. Clove had chosen to retire this year. Dad was on yet another trip, and the way she worded it made it evident that the journey was not as safe as it once was. Though, she made sure to say that he was always safe, and not to worry. And, of course, she gawked about the mentioning of me dressing up for a festival, noting that I should wear my hair up, so that I can "show off my elegant features." Her preference in this didn't change, which I found comforting.

Dee's note was simple. It outlined where we were to go to present, and at what time. I was asked to present last out of the four of us and needed to be backstage as soon as the first presenter takes the stage, so that I can get a microphone fitted in time. She also apologized, because this meant that I would be missing seeing most of the others' presentations. I was beginning to realize that I didn't mind all too much about watching the others, especially not Belleza.

As I stashed away my tiara and placed my dress back in the garment bag for safekeeping, I couldn't help but allow my mind to wander to Byrein. I felt the need to start planning ahead for his next move.

There was something I knew for sure. He planned on making sure that I joined him and the other Exes soon. How soon, I didn't know, but it brought an anxiety like no other to my soul.

Byrein's greed and desire for me was growing stronger, and I wasn't positive that when he came, I would be able to convince him to let me stay once more. Before, he seemed to be clearer minded, but now? His patience was wearing thin, and his desperation was growing.

I sat on the ground and prepared myself to check on Byrein. To gain any sliver of information as to a timeline for his next move. And more specifically: when I might be seeing him in person again.

Finding him in a Sight Episode was easier and easier, each and every time I set out to do so. Possibly because of the connection we share as fellow Mind Sights. Not entirely sure. But in a way, it made it less of a strain on me each time. In hindsight, that probably should worry me more than it did.

With a release of power from my knuckle just

barely brushing the floor beneath me, I eased into a Sight episode.

Byrein was outside of a tent. It wasn't his. He was standing and contemplating it. I could feel the tension in his shoulders. His power had grown stronger, likely from taking power from others.

I looked into his cold eyes. They were glossy with exhaustion. His scar on his jawline was barely visible in the dim, flickering light. He ran a hand through his hair, and in a way reminded me of Mr. Sean in the way he sighed when he did so. A few sliver strands caught the light, making him look even older than before.

A smirk spread across his face, though his mind seemed distant. "You will come join me, Esmari. You will be mine. I'm not returning without you. To live here another day without you. This time you will come back with me. You have to come back with me."

I realized, as he stepped closer, that this tent was new, with an "E" embroidered in the fabric by the opening. This was *my* tent. The one he had prepared for me. There was a lack of bustle around it. He snatched a side of the fabric opening and pulled it back just wide enough for the two of us to take a glimpse. The interior was fully furnished and looked inhabitable.

Slowly, Byrein slipped away from sight, and, before long, I was aware of my dorm room surroundings once more. I swallowed hard and started to make sense of just how soon Byrein intended on me joining him.

It was evident that it was sooner than I originally thought. His plans were coming together.

And my plans? Well, they had barely just begun.

Was I going to fight him on it? Maybe. Did I want to fight it? Of course. But something in me was telling me that I may not have a choice, no matter how much I hoped for one.

Would he kidnap me? I wasn't sure. Would he make it swift and secretive, or will he make it into a big display? Who knows? Should I tell someone? Who would I trust to tell?

I felt compelled to put some preparations into place now and prepare for the inevitable. Prepare for leaving, no matter how much I hated the idea of it. If there was one thing I knew, it was that Byrein would stop at nothing this time around.

He would watch the entire world burn if it

meant he could have me by his side.

fourteen

Over the next several days, my energy was spent on preparations for not only the festival, but if I was whisked away to the land of the Exes, fitting in lessons with Mr. Sean where I could. I began to think of what I would be saying when I presented, not just how my display would look.

I even went as far as practicing quietly in my dorm room. It felt very odd, so I didn't do that bit a whole lot. I hoped that I could just wing it like

Warren does. At least on the speech part.

I had prepared a few notes, too, in the evenings. Not just on things to remember for the festival, but also letter-like notes addressed to a few particular people, just in case I didn't have a chance to tell them.

I didn't want to be viewed as an Ex here in Banshui, though I didn't think that was going to be my choice in the end. None of it seemed to be my choice.

As best I could, I acted completely normal. I tried to make it seem like I was only stressed about the festival. But a small part of me worried that I wouldn't even get to experience that.

Though as the days grew closer, the more I worried that the festival was one of the last things for me to experience in Banshui. I wasn't sure Byrein would be bold enough to come to something like that, but at this point, I also wouldn't put it past his desperation.

Jewel seemed to do anything in her power to keep my spirits high. But I found myself almost at a disconnect from the joy and excitement for the coming festivities.

"There's going to be fun games and dancing if

you're into that. And I hear that they will even have live music this year!" Jewel noted, as we lounged in her room one afternoon. Jewel went to prop open her window to allow for some fresh air, before slouching onto the floor next to her bed. She pulled a nail file out and began reshaping her nails, preparing them for paint.

A voice wafted up into the room.

"—the festival coordinators decided to have me be the first to present at the festival. Daddy thinks it's because I can captivate the audience," Belleza said as she passed down below.

Jewel and I made a face to one another and giggled.

"When do they have you presenting?" Jewel asked, admiring her nails.

"Last." I shrugged.

"Save the best for last!" Jewel sang.

"I'm not sure that's the reason why," I remarked.

I looked over my friend. Her happiness emanated from her. She pulled out a small container of nail polishes and selected out two, bringing them one by one to her view.

Silently, she debated them, looking at the

shades as they reflected the light, admiring the opacity of the color. She ultimately selected a soft, glittery gray, replacing the other, much darker color in the box.

She slid it over to me and nodded for me to select one out as well. I debated the coloring of my dress and crown, and decided on a simple black.

She smiled. "I knew you would pick that one! It's new, and it dries extra fast!"

The peace was something I was beginning to know I would miss. The peace in these simple afternoons. The calm of the silence around us. No needing to act a certain way, or watch my back.

I wanted so badly to tell Jewel what I knew. That Byrein was going to take me to the Exes. That Mr. Sean was not as innocent in this as I had hoped. That I was supposed to be some solution to Byrein in his eyes.

I wanted to tell her how I found out about not just manipulating powers, but also about taking power away from someone. How I not only knew about it, but tried it and succeeded.

I kept quiet.

She didn't need to know. As much as I selfishly wanted her to know, the less that was included the better. Not just for safety reasons, but for complication reasons. But, to say it wasn't eating me apart inside would be a lie. It just wasn't fair to put that on her too. She would have to deal with the aftermath soon enough. And I needed to make peace with that.

We sat there and chatted about the little things as we painted our nails together, enjoying the warmth from the glow of the sun seeping into the room. We made plans for the day of the Regal Festival, how we would get ready together, and accompany each other there. We talked about what lotion we would use to make the day extra special. Jewel even had a whole "night before" routine she planned to put into place, so that she would look fully refreshed for a special occasion, such as this one.

Glancing at the clock, I stood with a sigh. "I need to bring back a book to the classroom that I borrowed yesterday. I don't want to forget about it. Want to come?" I offered.

"No, not this time. I think I'll stay back and make us some popcorn. Maybe get out a few face masks for us to do when you get back," Jewel noted.

I smiled. "Sounds good. I won't be long."

She waved with one hand and blew softly at the nails on the other. I waved back and shut the door behind me.

Quickly, I snagged the book from the desk in my room and was on my way to the Academy. In truth, I could have kept it. Mr. Sean probably wouldn't have minded much. It was a rather irrelevant book which he didn't ever look at, even Mr. Sean said so himself. Which is probably why he was fine with me borrowing it in the first place. He likely didn't care if it was ever returned to the classroom library.

I thumbed through the pages, taking a moment to glance at a small stamp in red ink on the title page. It noted that this particular book was donated to the school by someone named Yessonia. I continued through the book, turning to a very specific page. Page number two hundred nineteen.

There wasn't much on the page, much like the rest of the book. It was lots of boring material that had little to no relevance to Sights. Mostly things that came as common sense. Even I knew a lot of what the book taught, and I didn't even grow up around Royals.

But, this page, of this book, became the perfect

spot for me to leave behind a small note. Nothing too interesting, or descriptive. But a small something.

A couple of circled words in blue ink, along with a sentence at the empty space on the bottom and my name. Just a part of my preparations. If, or rather when, Byrein came for me.

It felt cryptic, and silly, doing these preparations. These letters. These little notes. This little crumb trail to leave behind of these things.

But I had to.

I couldn't trust that if I told Mr. Sean, he would do anything about it. At this point, I trusted that he wanted me safe, but needed me to solve his Byrein solution. The more I thought about it, the more I realized that I wanted to solve this Byrein problem too. In some way, that is.

I wanted my life back.

If I went through with telling Jewel, she would go to tell anyone and everyone. She would inform the Academy, her family, the ORP. Everyone. And if it didn't happen, then I would be made a fool. Or worse, she would raise the alarm so many times, about so many little things, that when he really did come for me, Byrein would be prepared to take out anyone in his way. By that point, everyone would think that it was just another false alarm, and honestly, who would blame them?

Mr. Higgens was someone I couldn't quite read. He was another that I could tell wanted the best for his students' long-term lives, but his methods were odd. He wanted to pretend everything was always fine. He didn't want to raise alarm and panic, ever. Even when he had the right information to make conclusions. He thought it best to take the chance that those conclusions are wrong.

He didn't mind experimenting, or allowing his students to experiment. He even pressured me to try something I knew would be dangerous with Mr. Sean, with the small sliver of hope it would be just fine. He makes me think that he knows more than he lets on.

The problem I was also beginning to find was that the ORP doesn't see anything as a threat until it was all actually happening. Lots of informational books and history books are always telling of how this heroic team of individuals is helping us as Royals stay safe. I am sure they are doing what they can, but they seemed to be always one step behind.

In their defense, having to weed out the false

alarms with actual threats, I'm sure, isn't an easy task. And the ORP has done many good things from what I understand. But if I go marching in and telling them that Byrein was coming for me, the only proof I have is that I saw it in my mind. Which sounds a lot like I have made it up. Truthfully, if the roles were reversed, I wouldn't believe me either.

So, the best option I currently see is to do these silly preparations.

It could all be a waste of my time, and I'll just dispose of them later. Or they could potentially be my sliver of hope, left behind for those around me. Either way, I knew I had to prepare, even just for my sanity.

I walked toward the Sight classroom, through the quiet halls. Most classrooms were silently shut down for the day. Several teachers had dismissed until next week, apart from a few teachers allowing for open lab time while they finished the routine paperwork.

Surprisingly, the loudest hall, I was finding, was the hall leading to the Sight classroom. Uncomfortably, I inched toward the noise, recognizing the familiar voices behind the chatter seeping from behind the closed door of my classroom.

"This is just what I am talking about! I knew you weren't ready to come back, Sean," Mr. Higgens scoffed stamping his cane down.

"Higgens, I did everythin' you asked. I took my time off. I cleaned up. I slept—" Mr. Sean retaliated.

"And you still came back with your old ways. Right into your old spiral. That child—" Mr. Higgens said.

"*Esmari.* She has a name. She's not just a child. She bears more on her shoulders than you give her credit for!" Mr. Sean countered. It felt odd, hearing him defend me.

"You convinced her to do the unimaginable. You are experimenting with her powers for your own pleasure. Teaching her just the same as when you taught your son. Nothing has changed."

Mr. Sean snapped, "Oh, you're one to talk! She told the both of us that usin' Sight and Sage Energy wasn't goin' to go well. You didn't listen either, and the both of us ended up in the infirmary!"

"It was *your* idea. If you didn't get your head on straight soon, who knows what experiments were going to be next? That child just, unfortunately, had to be caught up in the middle of it," Mr. Higgens noted fiercely.

"Caught up? Caught up? That's all you have to say? She was caught up in it?" Mr. Sean growled.

"It still doesn't change that you're teaching methods still consist of experimenting with her. Pushing her limits. What are you expecting from her?"

"If you were teachin' her, you would conveniently leave out these sides of her power, so that she can just discover them on her own. You would make her feel like a monster for havin' these capabilities. If *you* were teachin' her, you would just hope she never realized these sides to her power. She must be free to learn. This is a *school,* Higgens. *A school.* This is where she is supposed to experiment and understand her power. The powers that, might I remind you, she hasn't even had for a year," Mr. Sean sneered coarsely.

"Sean, you had her take someone's power. For all I know, you talked the child into it! How does that make you any different than that son of yours?" Mr. Higgens scoffed.

"I didn't talk her into it or convince her. I didn't even ask her to. The man did. He couldn't hear, so he signed to me. I just translated," Mr. Sean tried to explain.

Mr. Higgens sighed. "You could have left that part out."

There was silence for a moment.

Mr. Higgens was right. I wouldn't have known the difference that day. He could have made the man go away. He could have told me that the man was asking something else entirely. He could have told me the man was dangerous and to fly clear. I wouldn't have known. But Mr. Sean didn't do that. He chose to tell me the truth.

"The man found Esmari. He sought her out. And from what I could tell, it was not the first time Esmari had seen this man. He pleaded for her help. I made sure she knew she didn't have to. That she could say no. *She* wanted to help. All parties were mutual," Mr. Sean stated.

"You still had her take someone's power. Isn't that the start of it? Byrein spiraled after knowing that there was more. He spiraled into greed. Is that what you want? To train her to do the same? To train the next leader for the Exes?" Mr. Higgens demanded. "She took someone's power away, Sean! She stripped them of the very thing that makes them a Royal!"

"That's just it, Higgens. She took only a part of his power," Mr. Sean breathed. If I wasn't mistaken, Mr. Sean's voice sounded almost in awe of the encounter.

"Did she take it or not, Sean?"

"Yes, but not the whole thing. Not his whole power. He still has power. She only took part of it from him. *She stopped herself.* The control is unlike any I have ever seen. She said she took 'the part that wasn't right.' She left the rest. I saw it with my own eyes. He still had power when they disconnected. A power he could control at his own will!" Mr. Sean explained. The desperation in his retelling tainted his words. "You know better than anyone how difficult it can be to disconnect. You have said so yourself. You've said it's intoxicatin'. But she did. She stopped. She disconnected. And if I'm not mistaken, she didn't like the process in the least."

"The disconnect?" Mr. Higgens assumed.

"The takin' away someone's power part. She just wanted to help them *that much*," Mr. Sean said. "She's stronger than we give her credit for. She's a good person, Higgens."

"I just don't know what good it is for a child like her to learn to do those sorts of things," Mr. Higgens commented.

"I would rather prepare her. I want her to know about at least one of her powers enough that she isn't a danger to herself," Mr. Sean said.

"You are still holding out hope that she can help with Byrein. Does she know what you are training her for?" Mr. Higgens inquired.

Mr. Sean huffed. "You sound like I'm sendin' her off to battle."

"I'm not dumb, Sean. She may just think these are incoherent lessons, but I know better. I know you are trying to find a solution," Mr. Higgens prodded.

"I'm not gettin' into this," Mr. Sean scoffed.

There was another pause, and I thought about leaving. My feet were starting to hurt from standing on the hard hallway flooring. I could leave, but that meant I would still have the book. I could intrude into the classroom, but that meant they would know I was listening. I could leave the book at the door, but then Mr. Sean might look through it before replacing it on the shelf. So, I just stayed put, waiting for an opportunity to either slip away, or interrupt.

"Fine. Have you at least helped her prepare for the Regal Festival? Is she ready?" Mr. Higgens asked.

"She didn't ask for help. I didn't interject. She knows my thoughts on it. But it's something she needs to figure out herself. She has two powers that I can only pretend to know about. How am I supposed to know how to put them on display in a silly little show and tell session?" Mr. Sean grunted.

Mr. Higgens let out a long sigh. "Have you at least talked with her about it?"

Silence.

"A shrug. That's all. A shrug," Mr. Higgens scoffed. "Well, are you planning to attend at least?"

"I don't want to—" Mr. Sean said. I thought about the torture it would cause him to be around that many people. The headache it would cause him.

"Your student is performing, whether you like it or not. It won't look good if you didn't come. Plus, imagine how she would feel," Mr. Higgens coaxed.

"I just said that I didn't want to. I didn't say that I wouldn't," Mr. Sean said bluntly. "But don't expect me to stay long."

"Good," Mr. Higgens said matter-of-factly.

I could hear him come closer to the door. I knew I had to make my choice. Slip away or pretend like I just showed up? I took a breath and acted swiftly, taking several steps away as quietly as possible. Just far enough away that it would look like I had barely arrived. But not so far that I couldn't hear.

"Oh, and Sean," Mr. Higgens added, as I heard his hand meet the door handle, "make sure you wear something more presentable than that awful coat of yours."

"What's wrong with the coat?" Mr. Sean scoffed. I could tell he was just saying it to annoy Mr. Higgens.

"A lot!" Mr. Higgens stated flatly.

He opened the door, and I made it seem like I had just arrived, looking surprised. His eyes caught mine flinching slightly. I could see them formulating an excuse. It was obvious he had hoped the conversation was not overheard.

"Oh! Hello, child!" He nodded.

"Hello, Mr. Higgens! I thought I heard someone talking down here," I noted. "What brings you down to our classroom?"

"Just thought I would check on Mr. Sean. Make sure he was doing alright, after his return from the infirmary and all," Mr. Higgens said, not missing a beat. *He certainly is quick on his lies.*

"That's kind of you," I said.

"Excited to see what you have planned at our

Regal Festival! Please excuse me," Mr. Higgens said, bowing his head slightly and passing by me.

I allowed a breath to escape my lips before continuing into the classroom, book clutched tightly in hand.

"What are you doing here? Shouldn't you be gettin' all pampered for your big show?" Mr. Sean grunted.

"I'm just here to return the book I borrowed the other day." I shrugged, waving the book up so he could see the cover.

"Right. It wasn't that important. You could have just returned it next week," Mr. Sean said, eyeing me.

"No, I know. It was just in the way, so I figured that since I was done with it, I'd just bring it back. I was going to the store anyway, so I just wanted to drop it off on my way," I lied.

"Right," Mr. Sean said. He didn't seem convinced.

My mind raced. I could tell he was analyzing me. My words. My actions. Did he know how much I heard? I couldn't tell. *Think, Es. Say something else.*

"Actually, I was looking for an excuse to go for a little air. Jewel is bombarding me with questions about my presentation. I just needed some time to take a breath. She's making me even more anxious than I already am!" I tried.

Mr. Sean stuffed his hands in his pockets and nodded. "That friend of yours sure likes to ramble I've noticed."

Good, he seemed to buy that answer. "I'll just put this one back where it was."

"I'm movin' some of those to that shelf there. Just stick it right over there. On the corner shelf, next to those brown leather lookin' ones," Mr. Sean said, nodding me toward the correct shelf.

I smiled and placed it where he asked, making sure to prop it up correctly. I took a glance at the books beside it, taking a mental note in case I needed to take the book back.

"Okay, well see you, Mr. Sean," I said. I paused by the door. "Oh, maybe I'll see you at the festival. If not, I understand."

Mr. Sean glanced at me giving me no more than a grunt in response. I exited the room, closing the large, heavy, dark wooden door behind me with a thud.

fifteen

I woke the day of the Regal Festival with an uneasy feeling in my gut. An anxious bubbling filled every inch of me. Part of it was pure excitement for the day to come.

But I knew it was more than that. It was a calling. A beckoning. An uneasy disturbance from my Mind Sight. I knew it was something I needed to see from Byrein. I knew it had to do with me in some way. And I knew it was not going to be pleasant.

I glanced at the clock, in hopes that Jewel would still be asleep. Eight-thirty. Jewel was surely awake by now. And almost like her ears were ringing from me thinking her name, a rhythmic knock on my door sounded off.

I slid out of bed and snatched a hairband from my desk on the way to the door. Quickly, I threw my hair into a mess of a bun and opened the door to meet her giddy face.

"Happy festival day!" she welcomed cheerily.

"Morning, Jewel," I greeted.

"Don't tell me you just woke up?" she scolded.

"I was trying to get as much beauty sleep as possible. I've got to look my best today, you know," I teased.

"Well, I'm so excited that I've been up for *hours*. Honestly, I may need some extra caffeine today. I propose a trip to the Dripping Crown for some coffee before we start getting ready for this afternoon. What do you say?" Jewel offered.

"Sounds good, but I need to release some power, you know? A little tense this morning," I noted.

She nodded. "Understandable. You do what you need. I'll grab you out something to wear."

I smiled. I was almost grateful for her company this morning. Her joy and excitement were putting me and my wild nerves at ease.

I sat on the floor and adjusted myself until I was comfortable. Slowing my breathing and my heart rate, I pressed a fingertip to the cool flooring. *Okay, Byrein. I know you are talking about me. What is it?* I released a surge of power and launched myself violently into a Sight episode.

Within moments, Byrein was in front of me. He was reaching for something in front of him. A full black outfit came to view. It was sophisticated. Dressy, even. Complete with a suit jacket and cuff links, placed nearby. He ran his fingers over the fabric, examining it. With his cleanly buffed fingernails, he picked off the tiniest stray thread and flicked it away.

"Are you sure about this?" a woman's voice said. It was familiar. The same woman who I had heard by his side before, helping with the preparations for me.

"Are you questioning me?" Byrein sneered.

"Never, sir," she said softly.

"Good." He paused and looked down. "Did you shine up my shoes for me? They look like new."

"I wanted to be sure you looked your best when you arrived for her," the woman noted. There was tenderness in her voice.

"Make sure the others joining me are ready. I need this to run as smoothly as possible. I don't want any hiccups or attention with this. Esmari doesn't like that. No one approaches her except for me. She needs the comfort of knowing that she will be joining *me* home. She may not know it yet, but she will see that this is the best home for her. With me by her side from now on," Byrein breathed.

"I will be sure to remind them."

"Thank you. I know I can always count on you."

Byrein faded from view, and I sat attempting to catch up with my surroundings. My hand met my necklace charm, running it along my chain.

Byrein is coming tonight.

I was sure of it. Why else would he be preparing an eloquent outfit so meticulously? Would he be whisking me away before I could show my abilities? It seemed unlike him. Too obvious that I'd just disappear. Too public.

They would send out a search party for me. The presenter that disappeared. Flutters, Mr. Sean would do it himself. No, it would bring too much attention. Byrein was right, I didn't like the attention. All I knew was that I wouldn't be returning to the dorms tonight.

My heart fluttered nervously in my chest. On top of having to perform a presentation of power, on top of having to show to Belleza that I belong, on top of having to dress up and somehow function in heels, I now had to do so all the while knowing that Byrein was coming for me tonight.

I should have seen it coming sooner. Just like I can spy in on him, he surely could do the same with me. He knew this was important. He knew that I would be the talk of the festival. Somewhere I had to be.

But he also knew the crowd that would form. Best time to slip in and out unnoticed. And with me, no less. As soon as the presentations would be finished, the attention would move to the next thing. Whatever that would be.

People, Royals, and Accompanying alike would be talking about the show that we presenters would have just put on, but that's it. Just talking. They wouldn't be looking for us. I most certainly wouldn't be trying to seek out a presenter after the show, I would wait to see what was next in store to watch.

Mr. Sean was right all along, though. It would be the best way to show where I was. Display me for all to see. Including Byrein. And I said yes, anyway. If I hadn't, Byrein would be caught trying to find me in a crowd. Could he have still achieved that? Likely, but not with such ease.

I took a sigh and glanced at Jewel. She leaned quietly on the wall by my closet. She was relaxed, admiring her nails. Her freshly dyed orange-red tips, just brushing her shoulders with yesterday's curls.

Her blue eyes caught mine and she smiled softly. I realized that there would be no way for me to say goodbye without her knowing something was wrong.

"You okay?" she asked.

"Yeah, yeah. Just getting my bearings again. Thinking through things for today?" I said. It wasn't a complete lie.

She flicked her eyebrows at me, excitement glowing on her cheeks. "Yes! We have a big day ahead of us! Lots to do, so little time."

She helped me up with a grunt. "Hey!" I teased. "I know I've gained a few pounds, but come on!"

Jewel took it upon herself to pant dramatically, pretending to wipe sweat off her forehead. "I think I'm going to need an extra-large coffee after all this work!" She laughed. I shook my head at her.

Quickly, I got myself presentable enough to get going to the Dripping Crown. I found myself taking an extra look into the mirror, to check the smile I knew would be plastered on my face today, no matter how okay, or not okay, I was. The stress of the inevitable would be eating me alive, but I knew I needed to make the best of today. I needed to seem perfectly normal.

Jewel and I flew to the Dripping Crown and were greeted by a chipper Victor at the door, posting an early closure notice due to the festival.

"There, that should do it. Mornin' Jewels! Mornin' Es! I had a feeling I would see you both this morning!" Victor smiled, opening the door for us.

I smiled. "Thanks!"

Victor adjusted the wire-rimmed glasses onto his nose. He snatched his charcoal gray flat cap from under his arm and slapped it onto the top of his head as he joined us inside, slipping behind to the other side of the counter.

"What will it be?" Victor asked.

"Oh gosh, I just can't decide. Do I want to go with something chocolatey or something more in the caramels?" Jewel pondered aloud.

"Both?" I suggested.

"Wait! That's a great idea!" she exclaimed

"Okay, large iced chocolate-caramel latte, got it. And for you Es?" Victor said, ringing the price into the register.

"I never said iced," Jewel sassed.

Victor raised his eyebrows. "You yourself said just the other day that you 'can't have hot drinks on hot days.' That 'having a hot drink on a hot day is just madness!' It's a hot day," he teased.

"Well, yeah — but it would have been nice to be asked," Jewel mumbled under her breath.

I chuckled. "I'll have an extra-large of your blended cinnamon vanilla latte. With the whipped cream and cinnamon sugar topping, today."

"Woah, Es! Extra-large even? You never go all out like that!" Victor noted, scratching at his orange goatee.

"It's a special day. I'm going to need all the delicious caffeine to get me through it!" I shrugged. *Plus, I don't know the next time I'll get to have your coffee again.*

"That's right! *The presenter.* Are you all prepared?" Victor said, as he washed his hands and began our drinks.

"I guess we will find out," I commented mysteriously.

Jewel and I paid for our beverages and were soon on our way back to the dorms, making plans to meet up with Victor during the festival. Jewel and I parted ways to take quick showers and agreed to meet up in her room to get ready in a half hour.

When I had finished my shower and dried my hair, I gathered my things and entered the hall to Jewel's dorm, just next door. The chatter coming from many open doors on the floor was unlike anything I had seen since I moved in last year. Such a bustle about the day. All in great spirits. Some dorms had music playing, while others were filled with laughter and happiness.

I didn't know why, but I didn't expect it. The joy of the festival. Not the stress of looking perfect, nor the anxiety for the night to come. Not the snootiness of being better than one another, or to catch the right person's eye tonight. That was all absent. What was present was joy. Pure joy and celebrations. And it warmed my soul.

Swiftly, I knocked on Jewel's door. Without waiting for a welcome, I entered. I didn't need to wait. I always knew I was welcome here. Any day. Any time.

"Hi, Es!" Jewel called from the bathroom, peeking her head out of the opened door.

I stumbled my way in, with my bulky garment bag containing my dress suspended high above my head on an outstretched arm, leaving the door propped open behind me. I figured the music filling the hall was loud enough for us to enjoy too, while we got ready.

My crown box was perched in the opposite hand, with my shoes hanging by the straps at the crook of my pinky finger. Carefully, I launched the dress to flop across her bed, before setting down the rest, and finally retrieving my coffee from being pinned to my side by my elbow. With a huff, I nodded in satisfaction of my successful journey. *That definitely could have gone worse.*

"I'll leave the curling iron on for you, if you'd like, Es!" Jewel called, emerging from the bathroom, her hair twisted into an elegant updo, with a few loose strands curled at her face.

"It still baffles me how you can achieve such

perfect hairstyles on your own hair," I admired with a smile.

"My mom taught me a thing or two," she noted, nonchalantly. "I guess having a hairdresser for a mom has its perks. What about you? What will you be doing with your lovely locks?"

"I want it up somehow. My mom always liked it up," I said, smiling at the thought of my mom's beautiful face. I wondered for a moment how it might have changed since I saw her last.

"That's so sweet!" Jewel exclaimed. "Let me know if you need help!"

"Actually, that would be great. The last two attempts for my trial runs on my own did not end so great." I frowned. Jewel was much better at this than I was, and I couldn't pass up her offer.

"Best friend coming to the rescue!" she announced, snatching her comb and holding it high into the air.

I tried my best to explain my idea to her and where it went wrong. I apparently wasn't using the bobby pins correctly, or maybe it was that I was simply not using enough of them.

After a good long while, Jewel managed to wrangle my hair into an elegant and practical twisted updo, though I lost track of counting the number of bobby pins that went into my hair during one of her stories.

Jewel and I sat side by side next to a mirror, to put our makeup on. I decided to go with neutral tones on my eyes, nothing too overdone. I didn't wear a lot of makeup day-to-day, so I didn't want to go overboard. Though I did add just a touch of shimmer on some of my accent points.

Belleza's high-pitched voice broke through the music and tainted our ears. "I hope that Kasius knows which tone of my dress to match. He knows the colors of course, but I think if he decided to go with the deeper raspberry color, it would bring out the burgundy in his hair. It also would match better with the cuff links I gifted him. They are rose gold to match my crown."

I made a face at Jewel. She just shook her head before continuing to precisely apply her eyeliner. *So, Kasius is going with Belleza to the Regal Festival.* I don't know why, but it stung. I mean they were friends, after all. I didn't like her, but I also respected that there was more history to their friendship than just what meets the eye.

I had heard of a couple of people going together

to the festival, it wasn't uncommon. Especially, if you were already dating one another. So, two friends going with one another didn't seem too far off, I had to admit.

But I knew Belleza.

It was more than just two friends. Part of me wondered if Kasius was aware that he was going with her, or if she was just making it sound like he was.

You have bigger things to focus on tonight, Es. I stared myself right in the eyes and rekindled what confidence I had.

Jewel finished her makeup before me, leaving me to struggle on my own by the mirror as she got changed into her gown in the bathroom. I finished off my lipstick, just as she stepped out in her satin blue gown.

She looked so elegant and poised. Her high collarbones were perfectly accentuated by the single-shouldered dress, and I watched as the dress wafted around her. I was there when she had tried it on, but I was just as in awe today, seeing it on her again.

"You'll need to get going, if we are going to get you there on time." Jewel prompted glancing at the clock sitting at her bedside as she slipped a dainty bracelet on her wrist.

She was right, I needed to flitter a little faster. I stood and snagged my garment bag with my gown hidden away inside and my crown box. I had made Jewel wait this long to see both, and she deserved the full effect.

I disappeared into the bathroom to change, remembering at the last second to snag my shoes before I closed the door.

Carefully, I stepped into my gorgeous gown. It felt so natural to wear it, and yet I felt so out of place dressed in such fancy attire. The glittery organza fabric swished against the layer of fabric just below as I adjusted it to lay just right. I checked my straps and zipper, knowing that the last thing I needed for my evening was a wardrobe malfunction.

With gentle hands, I opened the box for my tiara, retrieving the earrings I had stashed away inside. After securing them to my ears, I lifted my beautiful tiara to my head. I allowed it to tilt back and felt as the prongs slid securely into place within my hair. I pressed gingerly to ensure that the piece would be at the ready, to last for all hours of the night. I slipped into my strappy heels and took a breath.

Taking a moment, I looked myself over in the mirror. With a small spark of Sage Energy flicked to my nail, I watched my wings fill out behind me. For the first time, I felt like I looked the part of a True Sage.

The sophisticated girl who looked back at me was not the same one who arrived in Banshui last summer. This was a girl, no— a young woman — who had experience under her. Knowledge surrounded her. This wasn't just some starry-eyed hopeful girl ready for an adventure. This was a young woman who was strong and would do what it takes to survive.

I adjusted my necklace and thought of Hunter. How far I had come since that girl who lost her friend. How much had changed.

I knew I would be facing Byrein tonight. And part of me felt scared to do so. But a bigger part of me had prepared myself. Prepared my heart for the strength I was going to need. Prepared my mind for the stress I was getting ready to endure. And if anything, I was ready to see him.

I was prepared to go with him, if I absolutely had to, that is. Because maybe I'd learn a thing or two about myself along the way. More importantly, I was going to learn about him. Learn his ways. I didn't see myself as the solution to him. But maybe I could find it.

I opened the door and stepped out of the bathroom, watching as Jewel's eyes fell upon me. I waited as she fought for the words to say. Pure glee danced across her face as her eyes soaked it all in. She clasped her hands at her cheeks.

"Oh, Es!" she gasped. "You look simply divine! That gown is perfect for you. Glen was right, dark colors really do suit you!"

"Glen's the one who helped with this one," I noted.

"I can't believe you found this one so late in the game. Es!" she squealed. "Oh, and your tiara!"

"I know, it's so beautiful, right?"

"Gorgeous. It's perfect. I just—I—it—I don't know what else to say!" Jewel stuttered.

"Wow! I think that's an achievement in itself!" I teased.

She ticked her tongue at me. "Seriously, Es! You look like a completely different person."

"It feels weird, doesn't it?" I giggled.

"Fantastic. The word you are looking for is

fantastic. Dressing up, getting all dolled up, becoming this whole other version of you that you rarely get to see. It's fantastic!" Jewel gawked.

"I suppose it is."

"And if we don't get our fantastic wings moving out that door, we really will be late. I just need to put on my heels," Jewel noted quickly.

"Right," I nodded. "I'm going to drop my stuff off in my dorm right quick, and I'll meet out in the hall."

"Okay, but be quick about it!" Jewel called as she began lacing up her first heel.

With a slurp, I finished off the last of my coffee and tossed it into her trash can. I rushed to gather my things and scurried next door to my dorm. I put everything neatly onto my bed. It was the only moment I had to set out everything I needed to.

My hands were trembling with a slight panic as I pulled the letters I had prepared out of a drawer. I laid them out on my desk, with the names of the addressees sitting face up and visible.

Each letter contained a note for the person it was addressed to, explaining briefly about my being with Byrein. Each letter also had different instructions of things I knew I could trust of the addressee.

One for Jewel, one for Kasius. Along with Jewels, I left a letter for her to find time to slip to Mr. Sean. And along with Kasius', a stack of premade letters for him to send periodically to my family back home, just so they wouldn't worry about me.

I had hoped I had made enough to delay their worry for as long as possible. Maybe even enough for me to delay it, until I found a way back, when I could read and respond to things they wrote me about specifically.

I hoped it all was enough. It had to be, at this point.

I took my dorm key in my hand. Glancing around the room, I sighed. I made sure that it was as clean as could be for my absence, and it almost looked bare and uninhabited. Quickly, I flicked off the light and locked up my dorm.

sixteen

We arrived at the Regal Festival with more time to spare than we anticipated. Thankfully, we did, because the main stage had been moved, as we were informed by a guard. Something about the stability of the stage, I think, is what he had said.

My heart was nearly beating out of my chest with anxiety. The decorations were grand, making me feel like some small nobody, from some small town, that didn't belong. Like I was pretending to be someone I was not. I walked cautiously on the raised brickwork of the pathway as Jewel and I made our way to scope out my meeting point for the presenters.

On our flight over, we noticed most of North District was decorated well for the festival. Though as we approached the location, just past the Ruling family's castle high in the sky, the décor became more elaborate. It was as if they built an entirely new, enchanting place, right inside of the Banshui.

It was already beginning to look crowded. Families were gathering with their young ones, likely looking for an early start to the festivities, so they could leave when the little ones got tired. Some students from the Academy were beginning to arrive, and I watched as a few official-looking festival workers were going through checklists at different ends of the space. I even saw several individuals with beautifully embroidered ORP attire taking their stations around the different areas.

The live band filled with all sorts of instruments had already warmed up and was gracing our ears with a beautiful melody. There were tiny lights strung in various plants, allowing them to twinkle and glow with a multitude of colors. The mixture of water features spread about, as well as the décor accented with actual fire flames, were all a wonderful display to see.

When we finally arrived at the main stage area, we found some seating, made of iron. Cutting right through the center of the grouping of chairs was a long pathway waterfall fountain feature, decorated with more lights and some mosses.

"Esmari!" called Glen as he approached us.

I smiled. "Hello!"

"You both look absolutely radiant," he praised with a glint of satisfaction in his eyes. He adjusted the cuff links of his navy-blue coat with one hand, taking care not to slosh his beverage, which he had perched in his other.

"It's all thanks to you," Jewel noted.

"I know," Glen said confidently with a smirk. "It's what I do. Make people look their best. Anyway, I must go say hello to someone else. Be sure to snag yourselves some of their sparkling cider before you take your seats."

We waved him goodbye and found the cider he spoke so highly of. Each of us grabbed a glass and wandered our way about the space, looking at some intricate sculptures placed on display by local artists that were tucked among the other décor in the space.

"Oh, there's my parents!" Jewel commented, waving her arm and sending some of her drink sloshing to the ground.

"Careful, Jewel!" I said, adjusting my dorm key, still in my hand.

"Oh, flutters. Sorry. Oh, they didn't see me. I'm going to go catch them before it gets too crazy here. I'll be right back," Jewel said.

"No worries. Why don't you find a seat with them? I'll have to be backstage anyway, and things will be starting soon," I suggested.

"Oh, that's right. Are you sure you'll be okay until then?" Jewel asked, inching away.

I smiled. "Yes, go," I shoed.

I watched as Jewel slipped through the forming crowd. In a moment, she had disappeared. I wandered about for another couple of minutes, taking time to finish off my beverage and return the glass to the appropriate area.

"Will everyone please make their way toward the main stage, our presenters will begin shortly," stated a voice over the speakers.

"Aren't you supposed to be backstage?"

whispered a voice into my ear.

Kasius appeared beside me, looking as handsome as ever. He wore a sleek, slim, charcoal-gray suit paired with a black button-down shirt under.

I noticed a lack of raspberry-colored accessories on him. No rose gold cuff links. No pinkish tie. Instead, he wore a simple, deep emerald-green slim tie. One that, if I wasn't mistaken, matched my dress perfectly. His hand met the tie's knot and adjusted it, just to be sure to draw my attention to it, no doubt.

"I'm heading backstage in a moment. Aren't you supposed to be wearing pink? You know, to match Belleza?" I noted.

Kasius shrugged with a smirk. He flicked me a look with a raised eyebrow that made my heart flutter. "Green is more my color."

My breath caught in my throat. Quickly, I looked away, so he wouldn't see me blush. I tightened the grip of my folded hands in front of me, and the metal key poked at my palm, reminding me of its presence.

I thought of the letter I had prepared for him, now wanting to change it. I wanted to add so many things to it. Would he understand? Would he be mad? Maybe it's for the best that I wrote it the way I did.

"You look beautiful," he whispered.

I looked him over and smiled. "Thank you," escaped my lips.

"Are you nervous?" he asked. I'm sure he was reading my expression, trying to figure me out.

I shrugged, sheepishly. "Maybe a little."

"You will be exquisite up there, I'm sure." Kasius reached up and fixed my tiara for me.

His dark eyes looked me over and I couldn't help but catch a glimpse of them. The way the light glinted off them. The glow from the nearby lights brought out the burgundy undertones in his dark hair. I looked down with an anxious smile looking at the key in my hand.

"What's that?" he asked, returning his hands to his side.

"My dorm key," I answered.

For a moment, I pondered. My original plan was to tuck it away with Jewel by the end of the night. Though, now, as I stood here, I realized that Jewel would know something was up if I tried to pawn the key off on her. She showed me numerous tricks of how to secure the key when you didn't have pockets. But Kasius wouldn't think anything of it. And someone needed to have it, as access to my dorm.

"Actually, Kasius. Can you do me a favor? Can you hold onto it for me? I'm worried that I'll lose it during my presentation," I asked warily.

He stuck out a hand. "I'll keep it safe for you." He smiled.

I placed it in his hand, and he reached inside his coat, dropping it into a pocket hidden inside the lining by his heart. With a pat on his heart for good measure, he tugged at the bottom of his coat and readjusted. I released a sigh, as I felt the pivotal moment where the plan for the evening was set in motion.

The lights of the stage came up and we turned our attention to the woman walking into the spotlight. She wore a ball gown that was hand beaded and looked as if it were laced with real gold. Ruling family guards stood at each of the corners of the stage as protection. The crowd hushed.

"Hello, all. I, as the current Queen of Banshui, would like to formally welcome you on behalf of the Ruling Family to our Regal Festival! It is all of you who make Banshui what it is, full of life, and power.

As such, we, along with our coordinators, have prepared a night of enchantment for you all, full of presenters and festivities. I hope you will enjoy yourselves tonight. Please join me in welcoming our first presenter to the stage. May you show the true heart of Banshui!" The queen gracefully exited the stage.

"And that's my cue!" I whispered to Kasius.

He glanced at me and nodded.

seventeen

I made my way through the crowds of people, all of whom were eagerly awaiting Belleza to take the stage. Her heels clicked on the finished wood of the stage platform as she took her place. Her steps sounded confident in the hushed space.

"Hello, all. My name is Belleza, and I have the honor of being your first presenter of the evening. I am currently still a student at Professor Javion's Academy for Royalty and am excited to show you all what power I am developing under the incredibly capable hands of our Head of the Academy, Mr. Higgens," she began.

There was applause, and she paused briefly to allow for it. I took a moment to look her over. Under her dazzling crown, her long brunette hair laid at her back in beautiful shining curls. The intricate beading in the shape of roses and vines in a raspberry color climbed the bodice of her rose-to-cream gradient strapless dress. It looked light, and elegant, and designer. Perfectly suiting her high-end taste and beautiful figure.

I ducked behind the curtain to head up the couple of steps backstage. For a minute, I just stood in the space at the top of the steps, attempting to allow my eyes to canvas the area before me. It was dark, and there were people gathered in small groupings, whispering to one another, taking care not to disrupt the presentation on stage. One person stood at the curtain with an earpiece, making sure everything was running as planned.

Dee caught sight of me and swiftly walked over, her floor-length dress just dusting the floor.

"Hello, Esmari. Here is this. It's your microphone. Go ahead and get that on properly. It won't be hot—meaning it won't be on—until you go onstage, so don't you worry about that. Other than that, you should be set. I'd like you entering from this side of the stage. Kat and Warren are entering from the other side," Dee whispered quickly, shoving a miniature box with a wire attached into my hands.

I nodded.

"Okay, I prepared that water in those cups over there for you, as you asked in your note. Do you need anything else?" she asked, glancing over her clipboard.

"No, thank you," I offered, as I took note of where she had set the water.

"Great—Warren! Kat! What are you doing over here? You need to be on the other side!" Dee scolded quietly.

"Oh, calm your wings, Dee!" Warren whispered. He winked at me, and I shook my head with a chuckle. "We just came to check in on our fellow presenter."

"Fine, but just make sure that you are back over to the *other* side in time to go on. You're up next!" Dee insisted. She glanced over her clipboard before scurrying away.

An expression of awe came from the audience. My heart felt like it was suddenly going to jump out of my throat. I was instantly regretting saying yes to presenting. I have never stood in front of this many people. Let alone had to talk to them and entertain them. I looked over the tan box in my hands, which Dee had said was my microphone, not knowing how to begin to put it on.

"Nervous?" Kat asked.

I nodded, attempting to look like I knew what I was doing with the twisted wire.

"Don't be nervous! You will impress everyone, no matter what you do!" Warren stated.

Another amazed gasp came from the audience.

"That Belleza sure is a piece of work. Impressive. Decent at her powers. But, what a piece of work! She marched back here like she owned the place, acting like I was below her. *Me.* A veteran presenter. I can see why you two don't get along!" Warren whispered. He took a chance to peek at Belleza onstage.

Sounds like Belleza.

"Here, let me help with that mic," Kat offered kindly, after watching me struggle once more.

"Flitters, I think she's almost done. I got to go,"

Warren breathed, he turned and pecked Kat on the cheek, careful not to mess up her makeup. "Wish me luck!"

"Don't fall on your face!" Kat teased.

The display of affection from him toward her caught me off guard. I hadn't realized they were a couple.

"You two are together?" I asked gently.

"We seem like an unlikely pair, I'm sure. But yeah. Been together for years. He's an arrogant idiot, but he's *my* arrogant idiot." Kat smiled.

Applause erupted from the audience as Belleza exited the stage. She came into the side stage wing and glanced around. She didn't even bother to look at me for long.

"It is so dark back here," she complained, turning away.

She pulled gently at the microphone and quickly got it off. Swiftly, Belleza wrapped the wire around the box and tossed it into a box labeled mic return.

"What are you doing here, Esmari? Are you lost?" Belleza laughed. She brushed at her dress and tucked a stray strand of hair back behind a bobby pin. Without another look, she exited the curtain to join the audience.

"She *is* aware that you are supposed to be here? She knows that you are a presenter, why is she so mean?" Kat scoffed.

I smirked. "She hasn't figured that out. She doesn't know I'm presenting."

Kat stifled a laugh. "Well, she's about to figure it out!"

"Yeah," I chuckled.

"Okay, now, if we tuck this box in at the back of your dress here, then it will hardly be noticeable. Just like that. Nice and secure. And here's my little trick. A small piece of tape riiiight here."

"Thank you!" I said, grateful.

A cheer came from the audience as I felt the heat from a flame glowing on stage. Warren had captivated the audience.

Kat gave my arms a quick squeeze. "Do me a favor? Show off a little out there. Make that Belleza jealous of your power."

I smiled and shook my head. "I'll try."

Kat disappeared to go to the other side of the stage wings. Another moment of heat and the audience clapped. I heard the sizzle of the heat meeting water, and watched as a misty fog filled the air. Warren exited the stage and Kat entered to begin her presentation of power.

I found it hard to listen, let alone watch her presentation. The lights got dim, making any hope of seeing from my position impossible. Every so often, a flicker of light would seep behind the curtains and the audience would gasp in awe or clap their hands.

I paced the floor, running through my speech in my head. I hoped that this would not be the day that my brain escapes me. I hoped my voice wouldn't crack and that my words wouldn't come out all jumbled. I flicked a puff of Sage Energy to my fingertip and allowed it to dance around my black painted nails.

Another bout of applause erupted from the audience for mere moments, before they were entranced by something else Kat was doing.

I wondered how they would react to me. Would my presentation be boring? It wasn't anything spectacular, like I knew the others' presentations were. I had planned something safe. Something comfortable. Something I knew I couldn't mess up.

I peeked out from behind the curtain and quickly found Jewel sitting with her parents out front. She was smiling and nodding to her dad to look at one of the rainbows of light Kat had created above them.

The audience seemed so serene. All eyes were on the presentation. Completely in awe and unaware of any troubles. I even noticed a guard smiling at the display.

But I knew.

I knew who was coming. I could feel it. Like an aching deep down in my bones. Somewhere, *he* was here.

Had Byrein come for the display? For the presentations? Or just for mine? Did he just slip in unnoticed, while one of the guards was distracted by the show? Or did he just blend in so well that they didn't suspect a thing?

No. I can't think of him right now. I won't think of him. Not now. Not when I go on stage. Who was I kidding? Byrein was always on my mind in some capacity. He was always lurking. What made this time any different?

This was my chance, my opportunity, to show him that I wasn't going to back down. That there was so much more to me than what he knows. This was my time to be confident.

Byrein needed to see that I am a force to be reckoned with. That I am not just some naïve girl he can manipulate. That I am unpredictable and powerful. He needed to see a sliver of my control. Just enough to know how miraculous and dangerous I could be. It wouldn't change the fact that he would force me to come with him. It wouldn't change that he will want me by his side. But maybe it would make him wary of crossing me when I got to his home.

Between Byrein and Belleza, I didn't know which I was hoping to show off to more. Belleza, on one hand, thinks that I'm too insignificant to be a presenter. I am below her and her family of solid crown Royals. Byrein thinks I'm too delicate and need guidance. That I'm some lost little girl, searching for his direction.

A humble applause, followed by some chatter, came from the audience. I glanced out to see Kat take a polite bow before exiting the stage. She caught eyes with me, standing in the opposite wing.

Kat gave me a big smile and a confident nod. I picked up a glass of water and allowed a shaky breath to leave my lips.

I was here to prove both Belleza and Byrein

wrong.

eighteen

I stepped out onto the stage, just as the lights were brought back up, careful not to slosh the water onto me or the floor in front of me. A hush came across the highly anticipating audience.

Quietly, I set the glass to the side and glanced across the audience, still surrounded by mist. With a smile, I knew my plan for my presentation was about to change. I straightened my shoulders and swallowed hard.

"Hello, all. My name is Esmari. Like our first presenter of the evening, I am also a student of Professor Javion's Academy for Royalty."

Polite applause welcomed me as I smugly eyed Belleza. I flicked a swirling ball of energy to my fingertip. I took a breath as I felt the release of power seep through my veins and radiate through my wings, as they completed their true form.

Her jaw dropped for a moment. Embarrassed, she looked around and breathed hotly, glancing at Lilly by her side. The revenge was sweet and so very worth the wait. A gasp rippled across the audience.

"I am a True Sage. I have two powers, one being Mind Sight, and one being this Sage Energy you can see," I explained, holding up my hand and watching for a moment as the colors flickering before it snuffed out, and my wings returned to their original shape. "I have put a lot of thought into this evening. How could I present my powers in a way that could not only entertain an audience, but captivate them? More specifically, how was it that I was supposed to show off my Mind Sight? It's all in my head!"

A few chuckles ran among the crowd. I walked to the glass of water and picked it up.

"I'd like to show you. Now, I know by now you

are wondering about this glass of water. Well, it did have a purpose, but I have a better idea, so—here you, sir, look a little thirsty," I handed the glass to a perplexed-looking guard nearby the stage. "Also, um, thanks for being here, doing your guarding duties."

Another chuckle danced through the audience. I gracefully returned to the center of the stage and took a seat on the ground. Momentarily, I fluffed my sparkly dress around me and watched the lights glint off the fabric.

"I'm going to tell you a little story. Unlike so many of you, I did not grow up here in Banshui. In fact, up until a year ago, I didn't even know much about Royals or these powers they seemed to possess. I had barely just gotten my wings. My mom was taking me on a girl's day, and we were getting all dolled up for it. Nothing this fancy—" I said, motioning to my dress. "But in the way you do in order to feel more confident about yourself. I was sitting just like this, the very first time I used my Mind Sight. Of course, at that time I didn't realize what it was called. It was completely by accident."

I looked around the crowd and caught Jewel's eye.

"Sometime later, as I began to explore my power and learn to control it, I learned that being connected to the floor was the way to go. Now, I realize that there is no way for me to show you what I am seeing in my mind. It's not like my Sage Energy. But what I can do is apply it to something you can see. I'd like to direct your attention to my friend Jewel."

Jewel's eyes widened. I motioned for her to stand up. Quickly, she bounded up and waved her arms. She smiled nervously at those around her, her mom beaming with pride.

"Jewel has no idea that I was planning to ask for her help. You see, as I was discovering how to use my power, Jewel and I came up with this game. She has the unique ability to use water, or, in this case, the mist you see around you, to form shapes. I use my power to see that shape. So, what do you say Jewel? Want to play our little game?"

She nodded and the crowd applauded.

"Okay, let's turn our backs to one another, so no one thinks we are cheating!" I spun smoothly to place my back to her. "When you are ready, let me know."

The audience chuckled, likely at something she

did. "Okay, I'm ready," she called.

I pressed my hand to the ground and released a surge of power, finding her immediately.

"A cube — a flower — I think that's a duck — your signature: Fog man."

I lifted my hand from the ground. Hearing whispers around.

"Okay, Jewel I'm realizing something. These people still may think we have this planned. I want you to go find someone, anyone, and ask them what they want you to make. Make sure they whisper it, so I don't hear it up here. Let me know when you are ready."

I heard some mumbles of satisfaction as she made her way through.

"Okay, ready!" Jewel called.

I pressed a hand once again to the floor. This time prepared for something more. A man stood next to Jewel in a maroon suit.

"A balloon," I remarked.

With a small surge of power, I sent my Sage Energy into the balloon shape, lighting it up the same color as the man's suit. A gasp of awe came from the audience, and I allowed the corner of my lip to curl into a satisfied smile.

Jewel moved on to another individual.

"A sunflower." I made that one pink, to match her dress.

"A horse." This time white, to match his tie.

"An umbrella." A lovely shade of aqua, to match their glasses.

"A cat. I think." Orange, to match her shoes.

Kasius came to view alongside Jewel. "A tree." I sent out a radiant glow of emerald, green to match his tie and my dress.

I lifted my hand and touched a finger to my necklace. "Thank you, Jewel. Let's have that be the last one."

A few disappointed sighs sounded in the crowd, as I turned and stood and dusted off. I watched as Jewel remained by Kasius' side.

"I used to think that my two powers were just that, two separate entities. But the more I learn to understand them, the more I understand what being a True really means. It doesn't mean that I just have two powers, but it means I have two abilities that go hand in hand. They work together, in harmony. Just like each and every one of you. These powers make me a True. They make me who I am. Just the same as each of you, Royal or Non, make the community of Banshui what it is. Our abilities and powers work in harmony, to better not only ourselves but the community around us. I feel the energy that each and every one of you contributes to Banshui. The way it connects us."

I knelt, closing my eyes. I felt the fog lingering around the audience. I felt as it wafted around their shoulders and brushed against the iron chair backs. I felt as it danced when someone breathed, and dropped as someone else adjusted themselves in their seat.

"Just like this fog, our ability is ever-changing, connecting us to one another. The fog you feel one moment, will soon move to another and brush against their skin. It changes at each encounter and embraces all of us. As if it wants us to feel as one. And I think that is the most magical thing of all."

I released a trickling surge through the fog, just like I had all that time ago in Jan's backyard. I opened my eyes to admire my display. Where there once was fog now twinkled thousands of colorful tiny sparks of my glittering Sage Energy. Gasps spread through the crowd.

Suddenly, one by one, the crowd stood erupting with applause. There were cheers and whistles. I looked at Jewel and smiled. She flicked a small tear from the corner of her eye and clapped her hands as loudly as she could.

With a bow, I exited the stage.

nineteen

My heart fluttered as I rejoined Jewel in the crowd after the conclusion of our presentations. She embraced me in a warm hug, congratulating me on a wonderful presentation.

"That was so amazing, Es!" she exclaimed.

"I was worried that it would be too boring. It wasn't at all like the others' grand presentations," I noted.

"It was different, and so, so good. Unlike any

presentation I have seen. And you let me be a part of it! Why didn't you tell me what you were planning? I could have prepared more," Jewel fussed.

"I needed you to be surprised. It helped with the show," I noted with a smirk.

"Okay, that's fair."

"I really couldn't have done it without you. Thank you, Jewel," I said with a warm smile.

The live band started up again. We linked arms and made our way toward the music to watch the band. I felt as something in the air changed, and I knew Byrein and his followers were near. I tried to stifle the sinking feeling in my chest.

Jewel and I found a spot near the outskirts of the space to observe the band and the groups of people beginning to take the dance floor. I looked around and caught sight of a friendly figure, indecisively wandering nearby.

Finn caught my eye looking, as if he were a little kid caught with his hand in a cookie jar. Nervously, he glanced between Jewel and me as he approached. His gaze wandered to Jewel more than to me though, I noticed. I couldn't help the corner of my lip turning up.

"Hi, Es. Your presentation was spectacular!" Finn greeted.

"Thank you, Finn. It's nice to see you. I'm glad you got the time off from work to come. I know working in the medical offices can be hard for that sometimes," I noted.

"Uh—yeah. My job isn't so important on days like today. I guess that comes in handy at times like this," Finn said, rubbing at his neck sheepishly. "Hi, Jewel. You look beautiful tonight."

Jewel blushed, tightening her grip on my arm. "Thank you."

"Uh—Jewel, I was wondering if you would like to dance—with me—dance with me, that is—" Finn sighed at his stumbling over his own words. I smiled sympathetically.

Jewel glanced at me, and I flicked my eyebrows at her. Ticking my head at Finn, I smiled. *Tell him yes! Go dance with him, Jewel!*

Jewel smiled gracefully. "Yeah, dancing would be nice!"

"Really? Uh—Great!" Finn exclaimed.

He reached out a shaky hand and she took it gently. Quickly, she looked back at me and flashed a giddy grin. I chuckled softly.

I observed the people around me quietly. Their attire, their demeanor. A younger boy came skippy cheery as could be. The band blended one song into the next as they continued to entertain the dancefloor.

For a moment, I imagined my parents out on the dancefloor. Mom dressed in an elegant gown, being led by my dad in a sharp suit and tie. I imagined them swaying and turning to the trills in the music. My dad would take my mom's hand and twirl her around, just like he had done so many times right in our kitchen at home.

My heart ached to see them here.

I got caught up watching an older couple sway back and forth to the music. They smiled at each other and chatted while they danced along.

Kasius walked up to me, hands tucked casually in his pockets. He was calm, and his stone face was happier than normal. Momentarily, he looked me over and allowed the corner of his lips to curl into a smile.

"Your presentation was quite the sight," he commented. I watched as his eyes glinted in the light.

"Thanks," I smirked.

"You had Belleza nearly fuming," he noted. I could sense a slight satisfaction in his smooth voice as he spoke the words.

"Yeah, I know. Sorry about that. I know you two are friends," I offered. Part of me didn't want him dragged into our silly little feud. But I still didn't regret any of it. Not for a second.

He shook his head and shrugged. Kasius seemed not to care. Though, when did he ever care when it came to the two of us? I think, though he didn't admit it aloud, he got some enjoyment out of my little surprise for her tonight. Part of me wanted him to confirm it, but I knew he wouldn't.

"Would you like something to drink?" Kasius offered.

"Sure," I nodded.

I watched as he began to step away to find a drink host.

"Kasius!" Belleza's voice shrilled, as she marched up to him.

He turned to her but didn't offer a word.

"I cannot believe they didn't ask you to present today, but they asked Esmari! It's just nonsense! You should have been asked! I would have loved to see you present. I mean, honestly! Esmari. Of all the students at the Academy, and they asked her!" she exclaimed.

Kasius tugged at the arms of his coat to straighten them. He offered her no response, but allowed her to finish, waiting patiently.

"Wait, why aren't you wearing the cuff links I got you to match my crown?"

He shrugged.

"And, Kasius, you knew my dress color. I told you the colors, I don't know how many times. Didn't you want to match me for my special day?" Belleza wined.

Kasius took a breath. "No," he said flatly.

Belleza's eyes landed on his necktie and flicked to his face in realization. He didn't offer anything more to the conversation.

Softly, he stepped past her, leaving Belleza to her own self-pity. She crossed her arms and stamped a foot down in frustration before marching off, tears welling up in her eyes.

I allowed a giggle to meet my lips and looked toward where Jewel and Finn were dancing clear across the dancefloor. Every so often, they would slip into view from behind another couple, and then disappear again.

The hair on my neck stood as I felt an unwelcome presence. I resisted a shiver racing through my spine. I stood tall and firm, unwavering in his presence.

"Hello, my Esmari," he said in a low, hushed voice.

"Hello, Byrein," I greeted coldly.

My heart pounded, but I kept my voice steady. I took a slight glance over my shoulder at him. He was trimmed and properly dressed. I recognized the collar of the shirt from my Mind Sight episode. If I hadn't known better, I would have mistaken him for just another Banshui resident.

But, I did know better.

"You don't seem surprised to see me," Byrein commented.

"I'm not," I commented flatly.

I fought everything in me to fiddle with the fabric of my gown at my sides. *Byrein will notice any sign of nerves.* I adjusted my feet for a moment, and calmly, I crossed my arms.

"You are the most beautiful one here. Your power has grown," he whispered, his warm breath wafting past my ear.

I offered no response.

"I've come to escort you home," Byrein sneered. His emphasis on the word *home* made me want to cringe. I stood firm. "You need so much more than they are giving you here. More than they *can* offer you here. A place to expand those growing powers of yours."

"What if I don't want to go?" I tested cautiously as took another breath.

"Esmari, I need you to look around," Byrein breathed into my ear. A stray hair dusted my cheek as he spoke the words. "Some of these people are willing to do what it takes to make sure that you, my queen, make it safely with us to your true home. If anyone were to stop us, they are prepared to act on my signal."

I watched as a man kept a watchful eye on Jewel and Finn, just at the other end of the dance floor. Another was moving through the crowd at a small distance from Kasius' heels. A woman sat alone sipping a cider within earshot of Mr. Higgens, as well as Mr. Sean. Another man sat at the back of Jewel's parents, as they stood and chatted with friends. *How many more were there?*

"I came prepared to escort you by any means necessary. I want you to come home. You don't belong here, with these people. This isn't the right home for you. It's not your true home. They are beneath you and your capabilities. Your little speech of Banshui was touching and all, but it just scraped the surface. We—I—can offer you so much more," Byrein whispered.

His voice was growing more and more desperate with every moment. He was growing impatient. I could sense that. I wasn't sure if denying him would set him off. I didn't know just how far I could push before he was triggered. *How many lives would he take tonight just to have me come with him?*

It was clear he was unstable.

I turned to look him in the eyes for the first time since he had arrived. They pleaded with me in the flickering lights, but showed so much desire. I could tell that he didn't know where the line was. He was willing and capable to sacrifice everything just to have me. I was afraid that meant that he would also be willing to sacrifice me for denying him once more. I wasn't sure he could take the rejection this time around.

But if I went with him. If I maybe made it seem like I *wanted* to go with him, maybe, just maybe, I could make it out of this alive. Maybe I could control the situation, not just here, but when we got to this home of his. It would have to be convincing. And I would have to decide right here and now, before his desperation got the best of him.

I had to try.

"Okay," I breathed. "I'll come *home*." The words were like acid leaving my lips.

Byrein motioned subtly to the others. Slowly, the Exes in view slipped away into the crowd. Kasius turned, sensing something had changed. He slowly looked after the man leaving his area. Even from where I stood, I could tell as he clenched his jaw. His observant eyes widened, and they met mine.

The world slowed down just for a moment.

I looked across the crowd at him. The burgundy accents of his dark hair danced in the light. I watched his chest fall as a breath left his lungs. His black eyes looking me over with concern, watching as Byrein stood beside me. I brought a hand up to my chest and patted my heart. *Use my key, Kasius. Go to my dorm. Read the letter. I'm so sorry.*

Byrein took me by my elbow and gently tugged me away.

Byrein smiled. "Let's go home, my queen."

A heaviness weighs upon the meaning of the word True. So often it is misinterpreted. Most everyone knows it to be the opposite of false or fake. But to label a person or a place as a true thing, or not, is subjective to the purity of the intention.

To be a True Sage, I needed to possess two very specific powers. Personally, I think that it's how I use those two powers together that honors the label True.

But when someone calls a home your true home, it brings on an entirely new meaning. When that person is someone you know you don't trust, the word True is now something false and distasteful. And the word True becomes the very definition of impure and of imperfect.

www.ingramcontent.com/pod-product-compliance
Lightning Source LLC
Chambersburg PA
CBHW051135190726
48290CB00006B/1850